MW00527085

Something
FORBIDDEN
KENNY WRIGHT

KW PUBLISHING

www.kennywriter.com

Something Forbidden

First digital edition electronically published by KW Publishing, September 2013

First print edition published by KW Publishing, October 2013
Printed by CreateSpace, Charleston SC

PROLOGUE

I nodded at the man's half-empty pint. "Refill?"

"No, I'm fine for now."

I knew the look in his eyes. He was a guy with a secret he was dying to tell. I've been in the bartending business close to 15 years—recognizing that look was second nature.

I cut right to it. I found that most people in his situation appreciated that. "Want to talk about it?"

The guy's brows went up. He glanced behind him, thinking that maybe the question wasn't directed to him. Seeing no one else, a smile spread across his face. "Am I that obvious?"

I shrugged. If he wanted to talk, then he'd talk. No point in forcing it.

Before he could decide whether to share his secret, a blonde entered the bar sporting the kind of little black dress I'd never be able to convince my wife Katie to wear in public. Her honey platinum hair curved around her angular face, ending in a sharp bob just below her chin.

I knew her look as well as I knew the guy's: she was here to get laid. And the man who got to take her home was going to have a very good time.

The blonde crossed the room, all eyes on her, including my own. She wore a towering pair of black heels that stretched out her petite body and made her legs look like works of art. She seemed impervious to the attention, although not oblivious. She smiled, tracing her eyes down the bar, where she met the man in front of me.

They shared a look packed full of meaning. They knew one another.

"Excuse me," I said to the guy, and left him to attend to the blonde. The predators were already pouncing before I even reached her.

Starlight Lounge was my foray out of the pub-scene. As the name suggested, Starlight was more bar than lounge, an attempt for me to *diversify my business portfolio*, as my accountant wife had encouraged. Callahan and Callahan 2 were both Irish-themed pubs, something that I was comfortable with. Their clientele was like me: thirty-somethings discovering what it really means to be an adult. Starlight's clientele skewed younger and more polished, a post-college group just looking for a good time. Like the blonde in the black dress.

A tall man—too good looking for his own good—stood at her side. I ignored him, focusing on the blonde. "What can I get you?"

She eyed me up and down before answering in a husky voice that matched her look. "Gin and tonic."

"Put it on my tab," her would-be suitor offered, turning his thousand-watt smile on the blonde.

I glanced at my friend-with-a-secret sitting at the corner of the bar. He was hunched over his drink, but was riveted to this encounter. *Curious.*

"I haven't seen you around here. You from out of town?" the guy hitting on the blonde said.

I suppressed a groan as I fixed her gin and tonic. Nice try, buddy, but you're not getting anywhere.

"That doesn't normally work, does it?" The blonde glanced at me, a half smile on her lips.

"What?" the man asked, confused.

"Your opening line. *Are you from out of town?* Really?" she said.

I smiled back at her, placed a lime wedge in her drink, and set it on the bar. "Gin and tonic," I said. To the guy: "On your tab."

The woman picked it up and took a sip. "Thanks for the drink from the town welcoming committee. Bye now."

The guy didn't seem to know what emotion to settle on. I saw confusion, anger, and then embarrassment war across his face. In the end, he settled on getting the fuck out of there, and left.

To me, she repeated: "Are you from out of town?"

We laughed. Already another man was making his way in her direction, this one tall, dark, and handsome. For his sake, I hoped he was wittier than the last. "You've got another incoming," I told her.

"Thanks for the warning." She winked and I preened inside at the attention, despite myself.

"Good luck." And off I went, checking on the drink levels down the bar. I was just out of earshot when I heard the new guy tell her that she looked familiar, and that he *swears they've met before.* I chuckled at that.

By the time I made it back to the guy with a secret, I'd started to put it all together, and he knew it.

"She's sexy, isn't she?"

"Very. She's with you?" For whatever reason, my pulse began to quicken. What kind of game were these two playing? I saw his ring, and a quick check confirmed she had one as well. "Your wife?"

"Right again, barkeep." His smile was proud, but there was a hint of embarrassment in his eyes. "Wife of five years."

I stared at the guy. He looked normal enough—attractive, even, with broad shoulders and a friendly face. He looked a little older than me—his late 30s or so—with a head of tight, curly hair just beginning to recede. He seemed like a family man, like me, someone I'd feel comfortable talking to at a barbeque.

And yet there was that edge...

"Explain that one to me," I said. The strangeness of this whole encounter made me bold. I would probably never see this couple again, so why not ask the hard questions? "You're married to a woman like that, and yet you're not over there, keeping the wolves at bay?"

He smiled broadly and nodded. "It's tough to explain..." He finished off his beer. "But I'll try, if you get me another."

I poured him another and set it down, leaning conversationally on my side of the bar. "On the house." *This ought to be good.*

He inclined his head in thanks. "I guess I'm one of those guys who gets off on his wife being with other men."

I'll never forget that line. He just came out and said it, leaving me blinking and stunned. I'd heard of the fantasy before, of course—even suspected that's where this was going. Call me naïve, but I'd never thought I'd witness it, and I'd never met a man who just admitted to it.

And as crazy as it was, I felt myself harden.

"So you like to watch?" I asked.

"Yeah, but that's not really what it's about. Not for me, anyway."

"So what is it?" I probably asked it too quickly. I felt like I was watching something on the Discovery Channel, not in my own bar.

"You're married, right?" He glanced down at my ring. "And you think your wife's attractive?"

"Absolutely." I thought about Katie, her auburn hair spilling around her bare freckled shoulders. All husbands are biased but Katie was indisputably attractive. I had the stares of other men to back me up.

Suddenly, it began to dawn on me where this guy was headed, and when it did, I felt my gut churn. He must have seen the look on my face because he nodded enthusiastically.

"You don't mind showing her off, do you?" he asked. "It's kind of validating, right? You have what others want?" He cocked his head in the direction of his wife, where a new man was hitting on her—this one actually had her laughing at whatever he'd said—in a good way.

"This is like the next step," the husband said.

"The next step after showing her off is to let her fuck other guys?" Despite my incredulity, I felt my blood pump hard. This was insane. I could never imagine Katie doing what this guy's wife was doing, right? And yet even my internal question had me hard enough that I was glad I could hide behind the bar.

"Can there be any greater compliment?"

My brain couldn't make that leap, but my body was already

way on the other side, racing into the distance. "I'll have to chew on that one."

The guy grinned. "It's not for everyone, but don't judge right away. Think about it."

"Hey, I'm a bartender. We don't judge. Otherwise we wouldn't be cut out for this job."

"Right on." The guy nodded. "Thanks for the drink."

"Thanks for the story."

I moved on, tending to a few other drinks, but my mind was on high alert. The blonde and her third suitor, a good-looking man still wearing his suit and tie, seemed to be hitting it off rather well. He summoned me over and ordered a pair of gin martinis. The blonde glanced at me without a hint of apology or shame in her crystal blue eyes.

"Thanks, Max," she said, reading my nametag. For a moment, I was at the very center of her world.

Then she turned to her latest Romeo and the spotlight shifted to him. I felt a twinge of jealousy I didn't have a right to and re-minded myself of my role as *audience* in these bar room dramas, not participant.

Still, I couldn't help thinking about my own situation. As I worked my way down the bar, I kept one eye on the blonde and the other on her husband. He didn't get up and make a scene. He didn't approach her at all. He just…watched.

I thought of Katie in this situation and my chest tightened. What if it was her wearing that tight black dress, enjoying a cocktail on another man's dime? What if it was her—my wife of over eight years and the mother of our bright little three-year-old—laugh-ing at a stranger's jokes? That spark of jealousy I felt a moment ago turned into an inferno, and yet at the heart of it all was something else. Excitement? Arousal?

I just couldn't wrap my head around it. Why would any man put his wife in this situation? I thought about returning to the guy and picking his brain some more, but at that moment, his wife stood up with the stranger and excused herself from the restaurant. The stranger summoned me over.

"I need to close my tab." A crazy wide grin stretched across his face.

"Sure thing. One sec."

I glanced at the blonde's husband, but he was already packing up his things. He'd paid in cash so he had nothing to settle. He met my eyes, a touch of embarrassment in his smile, and left. Five minutes later, his wife left with the stranger.

I'd seen a lot of strange things in my years running bars. I'd seen men fight over women. I'd seen women fight over men. I'd seen the beginnings of more one-night stands than I could count. I'd even seen a man come into a bar, find his wife flirting with a stranger, and accuse her of being a whore. But I'd never seen anything like I did that night at Starlight.

It did something to me. Changed me. Awoke something. Whatever it was, it made me feel ashamed. I wanted to bury it in the darkest recesses of my mind and forget all about it. Which is what I did…for a while, anyway.

By the time it resurfaced, six months later at Nadia and John's wedding, the roots were deeper than I could ever have imagined.

CHAPTER 1

"Nadia and John are getting married." Katie walked into the house holding up an invitation, the rest of our mail tucked under her arm. "That crazy plan of getting them together actually worked."

"You mean the plan where you eliminate the competition?" I asked.

"It's funny because it's true."

Mya and I were on the floor of the living room, building a farm out of a Duplo set we'd given her for her fourth birthday party last week.

"Who's Nadia Engine, Daddy?" our daughter asked.

Katie and I laughed.

"The little train who could not," I said. When Mya looked confused, I ruffled her hair and stood up. "She's a friend of Mommy and Daddy's, and she's going to get married to another friend of ours."

Actually, Nadia was more a friend of mine—by friend, I mean employee. She and I had been working together for close to five years now. She'd just come out of college and quickly showed a knack for running a bar. I put her in charge of Callahan 2 when I opened it three years back, and it was now my most profitable—although Nadia would say that opening a *trite Irish pub in a yuppie neighborhood* was the reason for success.

She'd also made no secret of her crush on me, and while having an attractive young Indian-American lusting after me was good for the ego, it wasn't great for a healthy marriage—especially with a wife coming off her first pregnancy.

It had been Katie's idea to introduce Nadia to her coworker, John, at the opening of Callahan 2. My wife hadn't hidden her rationale, either—*maybe if we get her to fall in love, she'll stop trying to sleep with you.* Three years later, here we were, receiving their wedding invitation.

We continued our conversation later that night. I was in bed. Katie emerged from the bathroom, face scrubbed, teeth brushed, and contacts out. Even completely dressed down as she was, wearing nothing more glamorous than a loose pair of PJ pants and a racer backed tank top, she looked incredible. How could she ever think I'd ever gamble all that for a fleeting affair with a younger coworker?

"You know, when you first set up John and Nadia, I thought it was a crazy idea," I said.

"Why? Because Nadia is a slut and John is such a nice guy?" Only part of her jibe was sarcastic. Sure, Nadia got around, but she'd call herself *liberated.*

"No. It's just that they're so different. Nadia is outgoing and… well, and a little crazy, sure. And John is so quiet. I always thought that Nadia would eat him alive."

"Opposites attract, right?" Katie asked. She opened her closet and began sifting through dresses.

"Is that what happened to us?" I asked.

Katie paused to look over her shoulder. "You mean the laid back restaurateur and the corporate accountant thing? Nah, that sounds about right." Then she went back to the closet.

"What are you doing?"

"Picking out a dress to wear, dear husband. Nadia may be the center of attention, but I want your eyes on one place only."

I slid out of bed and moved up behind her. I could feel her body heat against me through the thin layers of our pajamas. I kissed her neck. She smelled like her face wash, clean and familiar. Reaching around her, I dug into the corner of her closet and pulled out a dress that I'd only ever seen her wear in the bedroom.

"How about this one?"

"Ha. Of course you'd suggest that one," she said.

"What? You still have the body to wear it."

She'd supposedly purchased the dress as a Halloween costume way back in college, when she'd dressed up as a Playboy bunny. Like I said, I've never seen her wear it in public, and had my doubts that she ever had, but she'd put it on a few times here in the bedroom before deciding against it. The pale pink satin, fringed in faux white fur, was very tight and very short. Looped off the hanger were the bowtie and bunny ears that completed the ensemble.

"In your dreams, Max."

"Exactly, they've been in my dreams forever. Let's make it a reality."

The thought of everyone staring at her in something so revealing sent a jolt right down between my legs. Unbidden, the blonde from Starlight meandered into my thoughts. She'd commanded the whole room and her husband loved it. Thinking about Katie in the same situation—

"Mmm, feels like someone really does like the idea," Katie said. She shifted her butt against my rising erection.

"If you didn't wear the ears, it would almost pass for a real dress."

She fingered the white cotton tail sewn onto the ass. "I think this may work against its authenticity as a dress."

"Details, details."

We laughed.

I took hold of her tank top and pulled it up over her head. She wasn't wearing a bra, and her full breasts fell free.

Turning in my arms, she reached up between us and touched my face, the action drawing her tits together and pushing them up. God, she was just as beautiful as she'd been when I first met her, fifteen years ago. She was still in high school then, a teenager that a guy of twenty-one shouldn't have been lusting after, but I couldn't help it. Her red, wavy hair was a little shorter and a little darker now, and her hips and butt had filled out a few inches since having Mya, but the curves looked good on her toned body.

It had been a little too long since we'd had sex. What could I say? Eight years of marriage had taken its toll...

"Maybe I should just go like this," Katie said.

"Might be a little distracting," I said. I hooked my thumbs in her pajama bottoms. She wasn't wearing panties. "These pants clash with the rest of the outfit."

I pushed them off, the loose band dropping away past her hips as the whole thing crumpled on the floor.

"My stylist," Katie said, kissing me. "I don't know what I'd do without you."

I swept in, nuzzling her neck again as I kissed out the sweep of her shoulder. Palming a breast, I felt the heft of it before squeezing gently. They'd grown to a full C since Mya had been born and had only just begun to sag a little.

"I think you'd do just fine." If I weren't around, Katie would have no trouble finding another man to take my place. Not only was she beautiful, she was smart, successful, and driven. The thought of being replaced made my stomach tighten but inexplicably, so did my cock.

Katie's hands closed around it. For a second, paranoia raged inside me like I had a secret that Katie had just discovered. Only I didn't know what that secret was, and all Katie felt was my readiness.

"I love you, Max. I *need* you."

"Show me."

Her smile was all promise and wicked abandon. Rotating us, she sat back on the bed and reached for the waistband of my boxers. My erection sprang free. She grabbed it, feeding it into her wet mouth. My knees knocked as her tongue swirled me. Over the years, she'd gotten very good at oral sex. Within a minute, she was easing my length into the back of her throat. She looked up at me with those glimmering green eyes of hers as my balls brushed along her chin.

For an instant, my mind imagined those lips wrapped around the cock of another man. I banished it before it could take hold, but it was too late. My stomach fluttered.

Katie gagged a little as I jerked in her mouth. "I'm close," I hissed as my face burning. Ashamed, jealous, embarrassed—I was too many things to describe. Too many to deal with. She was mine and *only mine*.

As if I had something to prove to myself, I pushed her luscious body back onto the bed and spread her legs. Her breasts still sat high with only a little separation, giving way to a flat stomach and a trimmed, auburn bush.

She yelped a little as I crawled between her opened thighs and buried myself into her moist sex without further foreplay. She was certainly as ready as I was.

"God, it's been too long," she said, groaning as she slowly adjusted to my penetration. The first time after an absence was always the toughest, and every time I felt her velvet grip around me, I wondered why we didn't do it more often.

The answer, of course, was Mya. Or at least that was one of the excuses. She was asleep now, but it had been a point of contention in the past. By the time she was in bed, we were usually too exhausted to do anything but read for a few minutes and crash.

"Yes, yesss..." Katie cooed as I began to pick up the pace over her. She wrapped her long legs around my hips. I angled over her, drawing my heaving body against her breasts. Our mouths met in a sloppy kiss that neither of us could maintain.

"Come, honey." Katie dug her heels into my lower back. "Now... now..."

I held back as long as I could, but my imagination kept pumping that image of Katie doing this with another man. The harder I fucked, the harder it became to restrain my release. I pumped a few more times before I felt my balls seize up. Cheek-to-cheek, a grunt escaped my throat as I released everything.

Katie was not far behind. She arched her spine and pressed

her head into the mattress as she moaned. I thrust into her long as I could maintain an erection. At last, I collapsed on top of her, sweaty and exhausted—this time in the good way.

"Wow. That was hot," Katie said. "What got into you?"

I kissed her cheek and pulled the sheet over us. "I was thinking about how good Nadia's going to look in a wedding gown."

Katie swatted my shoulder, but laughed. "You know what? I'm going to need to get a new dress for this wedding. Nothing I own will do."

"You'd look good in a paper bag," I said, the teasing gone. "You're beautiful, Katie, and you're all I'll ever need."

"There's need, and there's want." She left the statement hang, then added: "And besides, I'm always looking for an excuse to buy a new dress."

****

As it turned out, her dress wasn't as scandalous as she'd teased, but it *was* new. Long and black with a cowl neck that showed a wider expanse of freckled skin than normal, it was also very sexy. She hesitated at the foot of the stairs, her toes pointed inward as I drank in her curves.

"Is it too much?" she asked, then immediately answered her own question. "I knew it was. I'm going to change."

I caught a glimpse of her back as she turned retreat upstairs. The sleek material hugged her voluptuous body, thin and tight enough to suggest she was either wearing a thong, or wearing nothing at all.

"Wait, Katie," I said before she could get away. "I don't think it's too much at all. It's sophisticated, like you."

She turned, regarding me over her shoulder. Her red hair was up in a high twist, so she didn't need to turn much. "You sure?"

The dress had a slit up the back, too, her nylon-encased leg parting the black material. I wondered if she was wearing panty-hose or thigh-highs. Katie wasn't one for fancy hosiery, but she'd been known to break out the sexy stuff on special occasions.

"I'm sure. And besides, we need to get going or we're going to be late."

Katie paused, weighing her options. She hated to be late. That she even considered changing now was a testament to her uncer-tainty. In that moment, I thought about all the other men watching her. I wouldn't be the only one checking out her ass out and won-dering if she wore anything underneath. That confusing tingle ran up my spine—the one that suggested arousal, even when it was so wrong.

"Okay, you're right. But I'm going to grab a shawl," she said. "Just in case it gets cold."

"Want me to help you find it?" I offered with a lusty grin.

Katie shook her head with a laugh. "We're going to be late—re-member, horn dog?"

****

I'm sorry, but here's a confession: wedding ceremonies bore me. I love the entrances and the exits, but everything in between is really for the two getting married—and maybe God, if you believe in that sort of thing. When I get bored, my mind tends to wander, and with Katie dressed the way she was and Nadia looking extra stunning all dolled up, it wandered into a pretty dirty place.

My first thought was about my own wedding and a younger Katie. She was just twenty-one at the time, beautiful in a cuter way, her intellect more book-oriented than worldly. I remember watching her walk down the aisle, resplendent in her long, white gown. I remember wondering how in the hell had I convinced a woman like that to marry me, and our convoluted history flashed before my eyes.

I'd met her for the first time when she was just 16. Even then, I'd figured she was way out of my league, and not just because she had a boyfriend who looked like a Ken doll. I'd been invited by a friend to his neighborhood picnic on the 4th of July, and having nothing to do, I went along. I remember striking up a conversation with her as we waited on the second batch of hot dogs, and being surprised that I could talk to her like an adult. We talked about bands we both liked (that I didn't think girls her age listened to), about politics and foreign affairs. I had to claim ignorance on a few pieces of subject matter I didn't know a thing about. We even talked about relationships, and how I was beginning to suspect there wasn't a girl I could hold on to. I still remember her saying to me, "You're all right, Max Callahan. I hope you find someone as cool as you."

I didn't see her again for three more years, although I thought about her all the time. She showed up in my advanced statistics class, a course I had to take for my MBA, and one Katie was taking because she was looking for a challenge. It was like fate; before, she'd been 16 and I was 21, but now, 19 and 24 didn't seem all that implausible. When I asked her out and she said yes, it turned out she'd been thinking the same thing.

I looked over at her now, studying the more mature Katie.

Her cheeks were more pronounced than that girl I'd first met, the cuteness of youth falling away to chiseled beauty. She had her head cocked to one side, her focus on the couple on the dais who were exchanging their nuptials. She'd always liked weddings, even if she didn't particularly like the bride for this one...

Which led my thoughts down a more lurid path. Nadia looked like a fucking model up there in her strapless white gown. Her lustrous black hair had been curled and constructed up and off her long neck and round-faced beauty. Despite her Indian roots, her parents had grown up in Canada and this wedding was a hundred percent Western. A few bright saris dotted the audience, but most wore black suits and formal dresses, like Katie.

I was attracted to Nadia. It was pointless to deny that. Even Katie knew it. But there was a difference between attraction and temptation. With Katie by my side, it was pretty easy to have one without the other.

"Do you, Nadia Bhatti, take John Mitchell to be your lawfully wedded husband?"

"I do."

The love in Nadia's words was almost tactile. I reached over and squeezed Katie's hand. She glanced at me, smiling back. Then returned to the exchange of vows.

My mind returned to its wandering path. To one night, back at the original Callahan, when Nadia had just been a shift manager with a lot of promise. I'd been working the bar along with her, but it was quiet so I'd decided to take off early. Only when I got half-way home, I remembered I'd forgotten something back in the office—so I turned around.

To this day, my ears still get hot at the memory of what I saw next. By the time I got back, she'd already closed down the bar and most of the lights were off. I entered the bar from the back, where the office was, and was about to call out a *hello* when I heard the unmistakable timbre of a woman's moan. I should have left at that moment. I knew all about Nadia's *liberated* spirit and she'd been flirting mercilessly with a patron all night. I couldn't not look.

Creeping down the hall, I saw them as clear as day. Nadia was splayed across the bar on her back, one leg looped over the bartender as his hips rose and fell, the other dangling off the polished edge. I drank it all in: her black hair spilling around her, her smooth, dusky skin, the way her breasts bounced with each thrust.

Fuck me, fuck me! She was moaning, her cries high and ragged like his thrusts were tearing them out of her throat. She arched up into him, her dark brown nipples hard.

"I now pronounce you Husband and Wife."

The groan of the organs broke me out of my revelry. Katie squeezed my hand, and when I looked over at her, my face flooded with guilt. It had been almost four years since that incident—Mya had been nothing but a bump in Katie's belly—and I'd never told her about it. She'd always been jealous of Nadia. Finding out that I'd watched my young employee climax on my bar wouldn't be productive.

The triumphant chords of Mendelssohn's Wedding March washed most of my guilt away. I decided to wash the rest of it away at the reception's open bar.

Some guys love dancing with their women. Something about showing them off, maybe. I don't know. I don't like dancing and it was never something the two of us did very much. Truth be told, I can probably count the number of dances we've shared since our wedding on one hand.

Katie, on the other hand, loved dancing. She'd taken lessons when she was a teenager for her cotillion ceremony (to give you an idea of what kind of family she came from) and honed her skills further in college at her sorority formals. I'd watched her plenty of times being whisked about the floor by random guys. I'd always just figured that these guys were getting a taste of what I had, nothing more.

Now, that simple thought was more complicated. I couldn't have it without thinking of the couple I'd met at the Starlight and the game they'd played.

From the bar, I watched Katie dance with single men eager to take her for a spin across the parquet floor. One man in particular seemed to keep coming back for more. He was tall and (in my opinion) generically handsome, closer to Katie's age than mine with the dark hairstyle of a Wall Street exec.

A pit formed in my stomach as I watched. It was a familiar sensation—you couldn't be married to someone like Katie and not feel jealous from time to time, no matter how secure our relationship was. Only this time, despite that metallic bite of anxiety, my pants tightened as my cock came to life. I watched her smile as the guy spun her around the dance floor and grew so aroused that I had to take a seat before someone noticed my excitement.

When she finally left the dance floor and joined me at our table, her arms and chest glistened with a layer of sweat.

"Having fun?" I asked.

"Never been better! Nadia now has a man to distract her from you, and she even threw us a party to celebrate it!"

That's not where my question was headed, but now that we

were on it…

"Give her a break, Katie. Nadia's a good person." I glanced across the floor, where Nadia and John were huddled in the corner, sharing a moment. "And she's in love with John."

Katie followed my eyes and sighed. "I know. I'm not being fair."

I pulled her into my lap and wrapped my arms around her. "You have nothing to worry about. You know that, right? You're my one and only. Forever."

She shifted, swiveling to face me. "Ditto to that. Want to get out of here early? You know how dancing gets me worked up..."

It was like a lance had struck me in the chest. What she said was true. The nights after she went dancing were always explosive in the bedroom. Now I was beginning to wonder if that had something to do with the guys she danced with. I thought of that couple at Starlight again, and the man's statement: *You have what other men want... this is the next step.*

"Let's stay a little longer. I haven't had a chance to make my rounds yet." I don't know what possessed me to say those words; they just came out. *Delay*, an insidious voice whispered. My body felt warm from the fire I knew I was playing with, but I pushed on. "Why don't you dance a few more rounds and I'll find you."

Katie studied me carefully, sensing something was different, but decided now wasn't the time to question it. "Okay, but if you don't come find me soon, you may be *sorry*!"

It was both exactly the wrong thing and exactly the right thing for her to say. I watched her float away and felt like I was floating, too. The confusing cocktail of emotions was so heady I thought that if I could bottle it up and serve it at the bar, I'd never have to work again. It was my first taste of that drug, and while I didn't know it at the time, I was hooked.

I found Nadia taking a breather by herself at one of the outer tables. It was so weird seeing her outside of the bar. Weird, but good. She looked good.

"Hey, kiddo," I said. I took a load off as I leaned on the table beside her. "Tired?"

Nadia looked up at me. A couple coiled strands of dark hair had escaped the high twist. One kept catching in the glossy sheen of her lips. I thought of Freida Pinto from *Slumdog Millionaire*—not for the first time.

She blew air at the errant coil, causing it to flip away momentarily before it settled against her slender nose.

"You know all of this is your fault. You and Katie." She said it with a smile.

"We're hopeless romantics who believe in love. What can I say?"

"You know, I never, *ever* thought that I'd get married. Being single's just too much fun."

She found John in the crowd, talking to some of her relatives.

"Now I'm part of the club." She held up her hand, showing off the platinum wedding band that matched the diamond ring she'd been sporting for the past few months. "Do we get a secret manual?"

I laughed. She was ten years my junior, but she was so capable of her job that I sometimes forgot about that. "That would be too easy," I said.

"Any advice for me?" she asked.

"Communicate."

Nadia snorted. "I've heard that one before. Cliché much?"

I shrugged. That answer *was* kind of a throwaway.

The crowd on the dance floor had thinned out considerably, but true to her word, Katie was back out there, fox-trotting across the floor to Sinatra with Mr. Tall-Dark-and-Handsome. Something squirmy started doing flips in my stomach.

"Who's that?" I asked.

Nadia followed my gaze. "Oh, that's one of John's brothers, Henry. Great dancer, isn't he? And cute!" She glanced over at me out of the corner of her eyes and added quickly, "But not as cute as John, of course."

I shook my head. Rings or not, she was still the same old Nadia Bhatti.

"I'm terrible, I know," she said miserably.

I gave her a smile and got to my feet again. "You always will be, I think." It almost felt fatherly.

Nadia laughed. I loved that laugh, and I was secretly happy that marriage wasn't going to change her, either.

"Nobody's perfect, Max. Remember that."

I nodded. "But we can all try?"

"Now where's the fun in that?"

"Have fun on your honeymoon!"

"Oh, don't worry about that. We will," she said, and for a moment, my head was filled with the memory of her getting fucked on the bar. "Thanks again for introducing us, Max. I better go make some more rounds."

Nadia stood, took a deep breath, and put on a wide smile. She didn't make it five steps before she was engaged in a conversation.

The foxtrot wound down. I found Katie on the floor, whispering something into her dance partner's ear. He nodded, smiled, and mouthed *thanks*. The first chords of Dream a Little Dream of Me began as he stepped away, leaving my wife on the dance floor alone. I took a step to join her when the groom, John, approached Katie first. He offered his hand to her. Her smile widened, she nodded, and he took it. My gratitude was two-fold: she wasn't dancing with Henry anymore, and I didn't need to be the one to take his place.

John was a couple years older than Henry, a little shorter and a little less dashing, but he possessed a quiet charm that must have drawn Nadia to him. Despite their differences, he was good for her. Being an accountant—an accountant on Katie's team—he grounded Nadia. Judging from the way he took charge and led Katie—his mentor and boss—across the floor, he was more than up to the challenge.

The song ended and at last, Katie emerged from the floor, her arm linked in John's. Oddly, unlike the display she'd put on with Henry, I didn't feel any jealousy. Maybe because John just wasn't a threat. It made me wish Katie could feel the same way about me and Nadia.

"Congratulations, John." We shook hands as Katie moved from him to me. "The ceremony was great."

He was too humble to call me on my bald-faced lie. "Thanks. It was all Nadia. Your wife has kept me too busy to even think about wedding planning."

"Hey now," Katie said with a laugh. "I granted you that long weekend that one time."

"Seriously, thank you both," he went on. "I never would have met Nadia if it weren't for you guys. And you two are an inspiration."

Katie squeezed up next to me. I suppressed the urge to kiss her, instead turning to John in thanks. "We've got a lot of practice. Just remember that it's a partnership and you'll do alright."

"Now stop talking to a couple of old folks and go mingle with your friends," Katie added.

"Thanks again for coming. I'll see you in a couple weeks, Katie."

He left us with a lingering smile. Katie hugged me close, her voice husky in my ear. "Now can we go home?"

This time, I didn't stall.

****

In the quiet of our car, as Katie pulled us out onto the highway, I realized how much I'd had to drink. The world spun around me, and that was more than just the speed of Katie's BMW. The disorientation was fitting—or so my slushy brain figured. It fit with the turmoil I'd been feeling all night long, that jealous arousal I kept going back for. Communication was key to a healthy marriage, I'd told Nadia, but good communication didn't mean divulging every thought and feeling to your partner. It meant being strategic about it, and whatever weird kink that that couple had stirred up half a year ago was not ready to be shared.

But I was drunk, so I started down that path anyway.

"You seemed pretty popular out on the dance floor." Acknowledging it out loud was even more thrilling than thinking it. "Particularly with a certain brother-of-the-groom."

I felt Katie's eyes slide over to me before returning to the road. "Henry. Yeah, he was a great dancer, wasn't he?"

"He was pretty good looking, too."

Now there was a smile with that quick look. "How drunk are

you, Max?"

My answer was as knee-jerk as it was false. "I'm not drunk."

"Oh, my mistake then." She giggled. "Yes, Henry was a cutie."

My jealousy started to surpass the inexplicable excitement I was feeling, but she went on before I could say anything.

"Did that bother you? Watching me dance with him?"

Somehow, I was able to rein it in and actually think about my answer. It was a complicated question—more complicated that Katie realized. The quick answer was that yes, it bothered me. Made me feel jealous and insecure. The rational answer was that it shouldn't have, that I'd always trusted Katie and her judgments. But it was the licentious answer that gave me pause, the one I didn't want to acknowledge. The one that said: it bothered me in all the right ways.

"It did. It's silly, I know."

I was surprised to see that we were already pulling into our driveway. Funny how space and time work when you've had too much to drink.

Katie cut the engine and looked over at me. Shadows played across her face in the darkness. She looked supernatural in her beauty: queen of the night. She was smiling—just barely, but it was there, an amused look that was more embarrassment for me than for her.

"What?" I asked dumbly.

Katie shook her head, but it only made it worse. The smile widened until I could see the whiteness of her teeth. She started to say something, but it was lost as she began to laugh.

"What is it?" I was agitated, but her mirth was finding its way through the cracks in my armor.

"Max," she said, "Henry is gay!" After that, her laughter was hysterical.

Henry was gay? I was jealous of a gay man dancing with my wife? Finally, her laughter caught on and I joined her. That felt good. Really good. I laughed until my stomach muscles hurt.

When it was over, Katie reached over and touched my cheek. "You're a silly man, you know that?"

"A silly man who loves you, Katie."

"I know."

"And you know that Nadia and I are just friends, right? I don't like her like I like you."

"I know," she said. "It's just fun to be jealous sometimes."

Well, that line certainly rang true for me.

"Come on, let me show you how much I love you!"

Before we even made it into the bedroom, we were all over each other. Like I said, when Katie dances, she gets horny. Couple that with the romance of a wedding and things got intense.

As for me, while the mixed emotions of tonight were confused, I knew for certain that something left me turned on. Katie noticed it, too.

"God, I haven't felt you this hard in a while," she whispered as she pushed her hand down the front of my suit trousers.

I rolled the cowl neck off her shoulders, baring the straps of black bra that had been keeping her tits on display all night long. I kissed her hard, my passion for her taking off. Aggression built in my wake.

"Do you know how many stares you got tonight?" The question emerged from my throat as a growl.

"I hope that some of those were yours." She turned, pulling me into the bedroom.

My eyes had been lingering on her ass all night. I finally got to reach out and run my hand across it, confirming that she was wearing panties, just really tiny ones. In response, she pushed the dress the rest of the way off her shoulders. The other discovery was that her stockings were lace-topped stay-ups.

"God, that's hot," I said.

She pulled me close and kissed as she worked off my own clothes. "I need to feel you inside me." Her voice was edged in desperation. She pulled at my belt, yanking my pants down even as she jammed her tongue down my throat. "I need it right now."

She shoved me back onto the bed and straddled me. Her bra and thong were gone, but her thigh highs remained. She sank over me, her pussy wetter than I'd felt in a long time. Something about tonight had worked her up. Whatever it was, I was benefitting from it and my alcohol-saturated brain was fine with that.

I gripped her hips, helping her rise and fall on my cock. Her full breasts shook with each bounce until she reached up and cupped them. Her fingers found her nipples, twisting harder than I ever dared to do.

Each full-bodied moan brought me closer to the edge. I looked up at her, her buxom nudity shoving me along. Her eyes were closed, her face screwed up like she was in pain. What was she thinking about? What was she imagining? Henry was gay, but had another of her dance partners crept into her imagination tonight?

She crested, bowing over me as she heaved out her orgasm. I came with her, exploding inside at the thought that maybe, just maybe, she was thinking of someone else.

How fucked up is that?

When she was done, she collapsed on top of me, her body on

fire. She ran her fingers through her damp red hair and gave a quick laugh. "That was fun."

Curling up next to me as the sweat began to cool on our bodies, and whispered, "I love you so much, honey. I'm sorry I get jealous sometimes."

"I'm sorry I do things that make you jealous." I hugged her close as I pulled a sheet over us.

"Me too." She giggled quietly. "No more dancing with gay guys."

I squeezed her close and shared a chuckle.

"You know, you had me going for a second there," I said, pausing. I was quiet, but my heart wasn't. It seemed to anticipate what I was about to say. "Have you ever thought about it? You know, another guy?"

"Of course not!" She lifted a little off me and I could feel her gaze boring down. I kept mine focused on the ceiling, not daring to look her in the eyes.

"You must have some fantasies..." I realized in that moment that despite the orgasm, I was still running downhill—faster than ever. Stopping wasn't an option.

"Oh, I see." Her tone changed to a flatter one. She asked her follow-up question blithely. "Do you?"

"No, no! It's not that. It's just...it's that...I mean, a fantasy's just a fantasy, right?" The faster I ran, the deeper I found myself. "Sometimes, I wonder that maybe I'm not enough...for you...you know?"

"No, I don't know. Tell me about that." Deeper and deeper.

"Um..." I felt like all the heat in my body was trying to force its way out through the follicles in the top of my head at that moment.

"Why would you ever think you're not enough for me?" she

asked incredulously, settling back down on my side. Curling her hand around my chin, she forced me to look at her. Her green eyes shimmered with earnest. "You're all I need. Ever. Am I enough for you?"

"Of course!"

"Then what's this all about?" She kissed me softly.

Suddenly, I wanted to tell her all about my odd conversation last July with the man at Starlight. I wanted to talk to her about the subsequent confusion. The uncertain arousal. But fear stopped me. Fear of being judged. Of letting her see a part of myself that even I didn't understand.

When I'd watched her on the dance floor with Henry, I felt like someone had hooked me up to a live wire.

"Just a stupid fantasy," I said at last.

Katie's eyes bored hard into mine. She knew me well enough to know there was more, but also that she wasn't going to get it now. She stared at me quietly for a final few seconds as she worked that out in her head.

"When you're ready to tell me, Max, I'm ready to listen. Okay?"

CHAPTER 2

As time passed, I began to wonder if I could ever talk about my illicit fantasy with Katie. Her family, a wealthy WASP clan from Connecticut, had raised her with a strict set of morals and I wasn't sure how she'd handle it. In a sense, she was too perfect.

Nobody's perfect, Max. Remember that. Nadia's words of wisdom; her way of preying on my insecurity, even when she had no stake in it anymore.

I'd thought about them often in the months since the wedding. No one was perfect. Certainly not me. And not my wife, either, although she certainly made her case. Nadia's words returned again and again, eating away at me.

I felt myself withdrawing from Katie as the season changed from summer to fall. Our nanny quit abruptly to go back to school (something she'd known she'd be doing but neglected to tell us) and we had to scramble to take care of Mya. I ended up working nights and watching her during the day, then switching off. When Katie traveled—something she was doing more and more of as her team took on clients of greater importance—I worked from home. We became passing ships, catching up only on the weekends.

Starlight was doing so well that I was beginning to plan for another lounge-type restaurant. Following the expansion plans of Callahan's, the second would be a little more upscale. I began polling the patrons at all my locations and talking it over with my friends.

It was Katie's idea to open a speakeasy style bar: minimal signage out front, dress code, doorman. It would serve fancy, organic cocktails and expensive micro-brews, and require reservations for tables. It was genius. Only, even as she explained this completely slam dunk idea to me, all I could think of was Nadia's statement that no one was perfect...

"Everyone likes the taste of something illicit," Katie explained. She was talking about the bar idea, but I couldn't help attaching a lot more meaning than that. "Absinthe is legal now, but it still feels pretty bad to be drinking it at an underground bar, you know?"

"It does..."

"When I was in New York a couple weeks ago, we visited one. It's brilliant, actually, from a business perspective. You wouldn't have to spend money on being flashy or any of that. This place was dingy, didn't even have a sign out front, and yet it was packed with a two hour long wait list for a table. The more subdued, the more authentic."

I'd always figured her company spent more time in boardrooms with laptops and spreadsheets than inside bars. My perception of her trips shifted a little.

"You already have experience with how to run a hip lounge," she went on, relentless with her idea. Katie always got like this when she was excited about something. "This would be perfect! Just what this city needs. And it wouldn't compete with your other bars. You could even put it next to Callahan 2."

Now that was a great idea. When it came to huge decisions like this, though, I didn't like rushing into anything. "I'll need to think about it, but you may have something there."

Took another two months before I had my business plan together and was ready to begin looking around for an ideal location. In the meantime, Katie's *everyone likes a taste of something illicit* comment ate away at me. I turned it over and over again, heaping on meaning after meaning until I was more confused than when I began.

Just as I was about to explode, *she* walked back into the Starlight Lounge: the wife of the man who liked to watch her get hit on. The blonde.

It was mid-October and the fashions had begun to cover more than they revealed. Still, the woman managed to look sexy. She wore skinny jeans that were tucked into heeled suede boots and a loose-fitting tunic that hung off of one shoulder. Her blonde hair was a little shorter than I remembered, razor straight but for a soft, inward curl that ended around her sharp chin. Purse in hand and confidence in stride, she could have just walked off a runway.

I looked around, searching the bar for her husband. I didn't see him. It was a little later than the last time they'd come in and the lounge was more crowded. He could have been here, but I got the feeling that she was flying solo tonight.

"Gin and tonic?" I asked as she settled into the same seat she'd been at before.

She had very well groomed eyebrows, which rose slightly in

surprise. "Sounds perfect." She cocked her head to one side and added, "Do I know you?"

Funny thing is, I felt like I knew her. I'd been thinking about those two for the past nine months. This meeting felt akin to meeting a star actor from my favorite television show. "No, don't think so. My name's Max."

"Chloe. Nice to meet you, Max."

"Likewise, Chloe." I set her drink down and she reached for her purse before I stopped her. "On the house."

Even if she didn't know I knew her secret, I was determined to show her a little celebrity treatment.

"Thank you, Max." She inclined her head graciously. Her chin-length bangs fell across her blue eyes. She flipped them back, a movement she had perfected. "I'd toast, but you have nothing to toast with. Let me buy you a drink?"

"Thanks, but how about I toast with water?" I made it a point not to drink at work, but this woman was shaking her head before I had a chance to fill my glass.

"That's not going to work," she said. "Anyone ever tell you toasting with water's bad luck?"

I slapped the bar. "Well, that explains a lot!" She graced the lame joke with a laugh over the rim of her drink. "That any good?" I said.

"The gin and tonic you just fixed me? It's passable."

Now I laughed and fixed one for myself. I held up the clear, fizzy drink. "Better?"

"Much."

"So what are we toasting to?" I said

She knocked her highball against mine. "Hm...Oh, I've got it.

One of my favorite things."

I turned my head questioningly, brow knitting. The mischievous glint in her eyes caused my pulse to quicken. "What's that?"

"Illicit sex." Her tongue darted out before tipping the drink between her pink lips.

I choked a little on my sip. *Illicit...* there was that word again. She went on: "When do you get off?"

"You're direct, aren't you?" I stalled, studying her face. She had a round face that made me think of Russian beauty queens, although she didn't carry even the hint of an accent. Her chic blonde hair made her seem sexier than the girl-next-door quality I'd picked up on before, but it somehow suited her better. "I'm flattered, but I'm married."

It didn't seem to phase her one bit.

"So am I," she said with a crooked smile. "What, don't tell me a hot guy—a bartender in a place like this—doesn't see some action..."

"Not this one," I said, although it was nice to hear a woman like this call me hot.

"Come on, really? You can share. I won't tell."

Was I actually feeling ashamed for not having an affair? This woman was too much, and yet I couldn't help but play along with her. "I'm not sure I can trust you."

"Oh, you can't trust me," she returned huskily.

"I get that feeling." I tipped the rest of my drink back and gave her a parting nod. "The answer is still the same. *Not this one.* Nice to meet you, Chloe."

"Likewise, Max."

It was surreal, watching her over the course of the night. She was rarely without a man at her side. She sent some away immediately; others, she kept around, toying with them like a cat with an unsuspecting mouse. I was mesmerized watching her work.

She had so much confidence; so much control. She knew she was the hottest thing in the bar, and that she could have any man she wanted. If only Katie could be like that. My wife showed glimpses, but she'd always been too damn humble.

I was on edge with her sitting there, knowing what I knew. My body felt overheated and agitated, yet it was one of the single most erotic sensations I'd felt in years. I likened it to my first kiss with Katie, or the first time I undressed her. Chloe was certainly not my wife, but as I watched her bat her eyes at other men, I couldn't not react like she was. And I had to continually adjust my cock, which remained in varying states of erection all night long.

As it got later and the bar's crowd thickened, I kept waiting for Chloe's husband, but he never showed. Chloe never appeared to be looking for the door, but it occurred to me that maybe one of the reasons she hadn't left with someone yet was because she was waiting for him.

Just after midnight, I saw that her drink and that of her latest suitor—a handsome South American guy—were getting low. "Two more of the same?" I asked her.

"I think we're all set," the guy said. He flashed a presumptuous smile at the blonde.

"Oh?" Chloe raised her brows and looked up at him. "You're leaving, Roberto?"

"I… um…" Clearly he'd figured he was going home with her, and was just now learning otherwise.

"Have a good night. And thanks for the drink." She smiled and turned to me. Dismissed, just like that. Confused and grumbling, the man shuffled away.

"Not illicit enough?" I scooped up her glass and began fixing her another. If she didn't want it, that was fine, I wasn't going to charge her for it anyway—hell, I don't think she'd paid for a single drink that night.

"Oh, he was fine," she said with a twinkle, "but I have my sights on another."

I shifted, trying to adjust my growing excitement without being obvious about it. She was too blatant to be successful with me—even were I single, she was a little over-the-top—but any attention from a woman who looked like her was arousing. I'd have to be as gay as Nadia's brother-in-law not to feel that way.

"You're going to have to relax your sniper finger then," I rebuffed, pouring myself a drink. "This one's not that easy."

"That's why I like him." She winked, stirring her new drink idly. "But really, I don't mind going home alone. My husband can take good care of me."

I shook my head, and asked her the same question I asked him so many months ago. "Explain that one to me. He knows you're here?"

She nodded brightly. "I probably shouldn't tell you this, but it was his idea at first. He gets off on sharing me."

"Like, a cuckold thing? Being humiliated and all that?" I asked. I went right for the stereotypes.

Chloe released a hearty laugh, covering her mouth when she realized she couldn't stop it right away. "I wouldn't call Greg a wimp," she said when she found her voice again. Her eyes went a little far away. "No, not a wimp at all. He just has some…peculiar fetishes."

"So you don't, like, tie him up while strangers have their way with you?"

She shook her head. "I don't think he's ever even watched, except when we swap with another couple."

My cock jerked again. Another revelation about my personal celebrity couple. It felt uncomfortable, forbidden, yet disturbingly erotic. "And it doesn't bother you?"

"Well, not anymore." She stirred her drink some more in thought, watching the ice melt in the clear liquid; she hadn't yet touched it to her lips. "It did at first, I suppose." All night, she'd been meeting my eyes with her own; it was odd to see her so diverted. "Like I said, it was his idea."

"How did he…"

"You're a curious one, aren't you? Looking to spice up the love life?" The confident Chloe was back, her stare boring into me. "We started off roleplaying it. I'd go in, pretend to be alone in some bar, and he'd hit on me like he was a stranger." She smiled fondly at the memory.

"You liked that?"

"Oh yes! It was really exciting. We did it a few times before he suggested I go in a little before him, let other guys come on to me." She took an absent-minded sip from her drink and answered the question I had before I even asked it. "Now *that* was a thrill. Gets me excited just thinking about it."

I couldn't believe I was hearing this. It went against everything I'd ever believed. Every moral code I'd developed. It both upset me and intrigued me. How could these two treat their wedding vows so casually?

"You should try it sometime," she said when I was unable to produce a response. She fumbled into her purse, withdrawing a business card. *Chloe Reynolds* was printed on one side of the cream card stock, along with the name of some commercial real estate firm. On the back, she scribbled down a second number. "My cell," she explained, handing it to me. "Either I'm a poor judge of my tolerance levels, or you're cute enough to make me forget my own rules—either way, I never give out my number, and here I am, giving it out."

"What's this for—?"

"Just take it. You're married, I get it. You love your wife. But you're also really curious about my lifestyle. Take it and call me if you have any questions." She slid off her stool, leaving most of her gin and tonic on the counter. "And seriously, try the roleplaying thing. I have a feeling you'll get a kick out of it."

With a final wink, she strolled out of the bar, alone.

****

When I pulled into our driveway, I was surprised to see the bedroom light was still on. At 2:30 in the morning, Katie was usually fast asleep. I thought I remembered her saying she had an overnight business trip tomorrow, so it was even stranger that she wasn't getting her rest.

I entered the house quietly, making sure I didn't wake Mya. I crept into her room and kissed her softly on the cheek. She was such a perfect little creature. Perfect and innocent. She stirred a little, crinkling her button nose, but didn't wake up. I stroked her dark, silky hair—thinner than her mother's, more like my own. One day, her beauty would surpass even Katie's.

I shut the door quietly on the way out and crept down the hall to the master bedroom. I wasn't sure what I'd find and for some reason, my chest was pounding. Chloe was still heavy on my mind.

Despite all the lights being on, Katie was fast asleep. She was wearing an oversized t-shirt of mine, her glasses, and was propped up into a sitting position on her side of the queen bed. Her laptop was on, but had slipped askance, half on her lap, half on the mattress, and papers were scattered in haphazard piles across the comforter.

In the corner, her suitcase was packed—a little Samsonite with wheels—and her dark business suit had already been pressed and was laying out. Organized as always. That was Katie.

I watched her for the longest time as she dozed peacefully. With her usually striking features softened in sleep, she looked like the girl I'd met in Statistics who'd captured my heart for the second time.

I tip-toed across the room and silently reached for her computer. The screen saver flipped off as I removed it from her lap, and a picture of the two of us on our wedding day greeted me. She had our digital album open. I'd already been feeling nostalgic; that discovery practically brought a tear to my eye.

Katie woke as she felt me over her. "You're home," she sighed happily.

I kissed her lips; they were hot and soft. "I'm home." I folded the laptop up and slipped it into her briefcase. She shifted on the bed, settling under the comforter as she watched me unbutton my shirt.

"I miss you," she whispered. "It feels like we've barely seen each other recently."

"Yeah. I'm sorry. When things settle down again, we'll find another nanny. You weren't waiting up for me, were you?"

Katie snuggled deeper beneath the sheets. "I wanted to see you before I left."

I pulled my shirt off and hung it up in my closet. My jeans followed next. I didn't bother putting on my pajama pants (the only thing I normally slept in). It was late and I should let my wife get her rest before her trip, but I'd been so worked up all night long. Sleep would have to wait.

Naked, I scooped the stacks of financial statements off the bed and set them on the floor before crawling under the sheets. My cock was already semi-hard (I wasn't sure if it even got softer at any point that night) as Katie watched quietly. She was beginning to wake up, knowing what was coming next.

"My breath probably stinks," she complained as I drew her against me. Her body was warm, a nice feeling after the chill of the night air.

"Probably." I kissed her. It did, a little, but I didn't care. Her tongue slipped into my mouth and soon, the (early) morning breath was a distant memory. I picked her glasses off and set them on the bedside table before returning to her lips.

She felt my hard-on against her stomach and mewed softly. I let my hands wander. She was naked under the t-shirt and her skin was incredibly soft. How did she do that? How did she keep it so silky?

Kissing her neck, my hands got a little more risqué. I followed the hollow that formed in the small of her back, tracing it beneath the t-shirt. It pulled up her lean torso before catching in the undersides of her breasts. I pulled away enough to peel the shirt over her head. When my lips returned to her body, they went right for her nipples. She held my head as I suckled, tasting the inch-long tip like it was a delicacy.

I switched breasts and let my hands explore beyond the softness of her tits. They traced the concave valley as her ribcage yielded to her narrow waist, then back out to her hips. I detoured across her buttocks: out and away, then tucking back in where her ass met her thighs.

I wanted more. I slurped off her tits and rolled her onto her back as I made a teasing journey down her stomach. I tickled her navel with my tongue, remembering the time when she had it pierced. That was before Mya; it felt like such a long time ago.

It was hot beneath the sheets, and hotter still between Katie's thighs. I spread her legs and propped her knees up on either side of me, creating a tent for me to do my work. The light was muted here, coming through the comforter reddish and soft, like the light of a photographer's dark room.

Katie had always kept her auburn curls trimmed neatly. Tonight, I could see the outline of her slit clearly, reading the tight-lipped furrow through her thatch. Were the hairs cropped closer? Was it narrower than I remembered?

I ran my tongue along her engorged labia, feeling the soft skin part as I prodded. When she got aroused, she blossomed and her pink folds emerged, opening beneath my mouth. I dragged the flat of my tongue up, crossing her slippery hood. Her body jerked. She gasped, catching herself before she could make more noise.

Katie loved oral attention, so I lavished it upon her until she was near breaking point. Then I introduced my fingers and that sent her over the edge. She was wet enough that I easily slid two into her, twisting them until my knuckles touched her trimmed pubes.

"Uh, yes..." she hissed, bucking up and squeezing my face between her thighs.

When I came up for air, she was still shuddering from the aftershocks of her climax. I rolled her gently onto her side and slid in behind her.

"You taste so good," I whispered as I guided my cock between her thighs.

"Thanks for that," she mumbled.

We began a slow screw, me spooning her from behind, her still recovering. I gently squeezed her breasts, staying away from her nipples, which I knew would be hyper-sensitive right now, and just enjoyed the sensation of sliding in and out.

I thought of Chloe again, and wondered if she'd been like Katie once: innocent, pure...she'd said it was her husband's idea at first, to go out and get hit on by strange men. Would Katie like doing something like that?

"Someone just had a sexy thought," Katie sighed, feeling me react inside her. "Tell me about it."

Could I? How would she react? I decided to tell her the truth—part of it, anyway. "I had a really interesting conversation tonight at Starlight...it was with a couple...well, kind of..." How to phrase this next part? "The guy liked to watch her get hit on by other guys..."

"Oh yeah?" Katie's voice was neutral. Unreadable.

"Yeah. He'd sit at one end of the bar, she'd sit at the other, and just let the guys flock to her."

"She pretty?" OK, definitely a little jealousy there. Proceed carefully.

"She never paid for her own drinks," I said carefully. "It was interesting to watch."

Katie was contemplative. I continued the gentle in-and-out of my cock and the tender caress of my hand. With my chest lining her back and our legs bent as one, we were as close as a couple could get. I only wished I could see her face, rather than have mine buried in her copper mane.

"You said you talked to them?" she said. Again, I couldn't read her tone.

"Yeah. They told me it was a game they played to spice up their sex life."

"So they left together?"

My heart skipped a beat. To tell the truth? I felt like I was already one step off the cliff; might as well jump. "No."

"Wow, I felt that!" she whisper-shouted as my cock swelled inside her. Was she mad? Fuck, had I screwed this one up?

"I'm sorry, I just...it's just a silly fantasy of mine."

Katie was quiet once again, her mind racing to process it all, no doubt. "I don't know what to say..."

"Shh...you don't have to say anything. It's not a big deal."

She hesitated. "Feels pretty big to me." She giggled a little nervously, lightening the mood. That was a good sign.

"Doesn't everything I do?"

"Mmm...every time you do it," she agreed. "I was looking at pictures of us tonight. I love you so much, you know that, right?"

"Of course."

"We...we need to figure out how to get ourselves out of this rut."

This rut? I hadn't thought about it like that. We were missing one another, sure, but that was just the situation, right?

"But I don't know if I can do what you are suggesting..."

"Oh, no! I didn't bring it up to...I mean, it's just a fantasy. I don't think I could—" My face burned. I repeated myself. "It's just a fantasy."

Katie relaxed in my arms; I didn't realize she'd been tense. I guess I was, too.

"Thank God." She laughed in relief. "I don't think you could handle me doing something like that...I mean, you've always been a little jealous and...it was just a surprise to hear..."

"Yeah, just a fantasy," I reassured. "Although maybe we could try role-playing? Once or twice, you know? Like you and I pretend to be strangers."

"That could be fun. You could be the bartender, trying to pick up a lonely woman at the bar."

"Now that would really be fiction."

Katie laughed. "It better be!" I began to fuck her a little quicker as our conversation changed. "Or, you could be a stranger, slipping into bed with a lonely wife."

"A little far-fetched, but I like your thinking..."

I let her think. Let her work this one out. "Maybe this is my last night in New York," she suggested. She'd be there tomorrow. Now she was getting into the fantasy. "And you're a stranger I picked up at the hotel bar."

I moved my hand off her breast and clutched her hip. Leveraging inside her, I began to fuck her even faster.

"God, baby, that feels so good," she whimpered. "A little harder—AH!"

She bit down, stifling the throaty gasp.

This felt so different. So good. My voice trembled. "Did you flirt with anyone else before I picked you up?"

"A couple guys, but you were definitely the cutest."

Oh God. I wasn't going to be able to take much more of this. "So you went in there, looking for someone to hook up with?"

She bent forward a little, our skin-on-skin contact breaking as she found a better angle to receive my thrusts. "Honey, uhhh..." she moaned. The sheets whisked beneath our undulating bodies, the friction causing a searing lick of heat along my hip. "No...I never intended to...yes, fuck...I'm married and I've never...never..."

"Never been hit on by a stranger?"

"No. Yes. I mean, that happens all the time..."

Christ, she knew how to tease me! I rolled her onto her front and got low between her legs. I fucked her in some kind of flattened out doggy style. Katie buried her face in the pillow, her cries turning more passionate.

"I'm the first guy who's ever been successful," I groaned, plugging my cock harder and harder into her wet slit. Each thrust brought me down hard against the firm surface of her buttocks.

"Yeah... yeah! YEAH!" she cried into the pillow, shoving her ass up into the air as she came. I was right behind her, releasing everything I had into her depths. Was Katie thinking of me as she came? Or the stranger?

Either way, she reminded me, once again, how great she was.

CHAPTER 3

Two weekends later, Halloween weekend, was one of those rare weekends in which both Katie and I were home at the same time. Mya was only four, so while we'd dress her up and take her out somewhere, she was still too young to stay up late.

As the day approached, I asked off-handedly what kind of sexy costume Katie was going to get. Predictably, she just rolled her eyes and ignored the comment.

"We should go out," I suggested, feeling compelled to push a little. "Get a sitter to watch Mya when she goes to bed and, I don't know..."

"Hit some bars?" Katie laughed. "Don't you think we're a little too old for that?"

"Only as old as you feel. Come on, it'll be fun."

"You just want me to dress up as some sexy nurse or some-thing."

"Not necessarily. You could go as a sexy ghost, a sexy witch,"

I said, ticking each option off in my hand, "a sexy school girl, a sexy—"

"Alright, alright, horn dog! I get it." At least she was laughing.

"So, sexy horn dog? I don't know about that—"

Katie rolled her eyes and laughed. "I'll horn dog you!"

Now would have been a great time to bring up the conversation we still hadn't had: the follow-up to the night I'd come home from the bar and fucked her as a stranger. But I couldn't form the words.

The next couple weeks crawled. I knew that Halloween would probably be as tame as ever. Last year, Katie had dressed up as a witch (and not the sexy kind). The year before that, she'd been an elf from *Lord of the Rings*, which was cool, just not erotic. I wasn't expecting much, but they say hope springs eternal.

More than that, though, I wanted to see Katie step out of her shell again; I wanted to find that vibrant, sexy creature who'd come up with the stranger-in-the-hotel scenario.

I began to hatch a plan.

On Halloween, I made sure to shift my schedules around so that I had to "cover" for one of my managers who wanted to go out with his kids (older than Mya, in the age range when trick-or-treating was a parent-child event). The plan was to meet Katie at Champs-Élysées, an upscale, French-themed bistro-and-bar on the other side of town. I'd learned through my contacts that it had a pretty raucous Halloween party and the age range was in the 30s. Perfect.

Callahan's (the original location) was packed that night, and I ended up covering bar—or wherever else needed it. Like the rest of the employees, I made sure to come dressed up, my costume being a grim reaper get-up complete with hooded cloak and tall, plastic scythe. I even put a little face paint on, giving me a pallid complexion appropriate for Death.

At 10:00, when I was supposed to be heading out, I texted Katie telling her as much. My plan was to delay a little, let her get there before me and have a chance to mingle, and then arrive. Hopefully she'd loosen up, have a few drinks, flirt with a few guys—the thought alone had my heart going—then I could arrive, pretend to pick her up, and hopefully she'd play along.

I ended up getting delayed for real when we had a fight break out between two guys who'd had too much to drink. I had to wait for the cops to arrive and sort it out, ignoring my wife's periodic texts of *Where the hell are you?!* until I was finally able to leave.

Sorry, delayed. On the way now! I texted at last. It was nearly 10:45. By the time I actually got through the annoyingly long line at Champs-Élysées, it was after 11. Not good at all.

The first thing I noticed about the bar was that it was loud. Wall of sound in the face loud. The two story-tall ceilings had something to do with it, sure, but so did the at-capacity crowd. No wonder there was a line. A DJ was spinning something with dance beats and nearly unintelligible French lyrics, and a large portion of the bistro-style joint was now serving as a dance floor.

Everyone was dressed in some Halloween costume. Some were clever—a man dressed as Justin Timberlake's SNL Dick in a Box, for example—but most were generic. For men, that meant costumes like mine. For women, fortunately, it meant something verging on slutty.

As soon as I was in, I scanned the bar, searching for Katie. There were so many people and so much movement that I wasn't sure I'd be successful. I pulled my phone out to text her when I spotted her, standing at the corner of the bar on the far side. My jaw dropped.

The pale pink Playboy bunny costume had made it out of the bedroom for the first time in over nine years. She wore it with the bunny ears and the choker collar and bowtie, and as I stepped closer, I noticed that she'd paired it with a pair of tall platform heels that I didn't recognize.

Not only that, she wasn't alone.

The guy, dressed as some kind of pirate, leaned close, and whispered something into her ear. His eyes darted down the front of her outfit, where her full tits spilled over the top of the white satin. Katie actually scanned the entrance before answering, looking for me, perhaps? Unbelievably, her eyes passed right by me.

At first, I was confused. Had she not seen me? Or had she read my mind and decided to toy with me a little? I dismissed that one right away, and a second later realized that she probably didn't recognize me with my grim reaper hood up. With a little bit of hesitation, she nodded to the guy and let herself be led onto the dance floor.

God, her pink, satin outfit was short! Her modesty was only marginally protected by the addition of the ruffled tutu hem.

It was as though someone had just plugged me into the mains. I was barely able to reach the bar. The dense crowd didn't even register; I may as well have been in an empty room. I ordered a double shot of bourbon, neat, and downed nearly all of it on one go. I moved close enough to watch her shimmy and shake with the stranger, feeling simultaneously sick to my stomach and as turned on as I'd ever been in my life, and judging by her face, she wasn't even into him! Imagine if she was…

No, not going there. Not tonight. He started to get a little handsy, moving down her back to the taut padding of her buttocks. She removed them promptly, but he was persistent. She needed rescuing and it was time for another "stranger" to help her out.

Wiping the bourbon from my lips, I shoved my way onto the dance floor and tapped the guy on the shoulder. He glanced around at me, shrugged, and decided to ignore my presence. I tapped his shoulder again. "What's your problem, man?"

"Mind if I cut in?" I asked, ignoring his aggression.

"Fuck yeah, I mind. You her husband or something?"

Katie's eyes filled with relief, not to mention a little bit of amusement at the situation. "Nope, just a guy she'd rather dance with. Am I right, honey-bunny?" Katie laughed at that one. God bless her for laughing at my jokes. "I'm Grim, by the way. You are…"

More laughter. "Call me Bunny."

The pirate fumed beside us as we ignored him. At last, I turned to him. "Two options, Buccaneer Bob. You can make a scene, humiliate yourself a little bit more—and ruin any chances you have of getting laid tonight—or you could move on. I suggest the latter."

He balled his fists up and, for a moment, I thought he was going to hit me. Then, all the air seemed to leave him like a rapidly deflating balloon. "She's a slut anyway," he muttered beneath his breath as he stormed off, heading back to the bar.

"Well done, *Grim*." Katie giggled. We began to dance. She leaned close to me, whispering, "I wasn't sure how to get rid of him myself."

She smelled good, wearing some kind of perfume I associated with date nights and formal events. It always reminded me of sex.

"Can't really blame him." I slid my hand along the contours of her back and hip. "You're a pretty tempting sight."

She grabbed my hand just as it began to curve around her buttocks and put it back to somewhere decent. She really was getting it! My cock grew harder. "Oh, this old thing? Just something I had in the back of my closet for special occasions."

She stood back and posed for me. I ran my eyes along her curves, amazed that she was dressed in public like that. God bless this holiday! The strapless, satin dress was plastered to her curves and was tight like a corset. Long, black satin gloves and a choker with a bow tie on it matched the bunny ear accessories.

"Your husband, huh? He around?"

Her green eyes flashed as we both realized we were okay with this game. "He was supposed to meet me here, but he hasn't been answering my texts." Dressed up as a Playboy bunny, her pout was priceless.

"Well, Bunny, why not flirt a little with Death while you wait?"

"Mmm," she whispered, sidling back up to me as we danced. Her hand found the front opening of my cloak. I jumped as her hand closed over my erection. She squeezed me, giggling. "That a euphemism for sex?"

In the crowd, no one was the wiser, but Katie was definitely being bolder than usual. I wondered how much she'd had to drink before I got here.

"Can be," I croaked. Suddenly we really were strangers—Katie the hot vixen, me the uncertain boy, the putty in her very warm hands.

I wrapped my arms around her, feeling her breasts against my chest. I rested my hands on her hips as she sashayed to the French euro-beat, and pulled her closer. She slid her hands out of my robes and up to my face.

"I'm having fun," she whispered. Her face was alive and smiling. I wanted to remember her like that forever: the picture of happiness.

"You're incredible. You can't be my wife because she'd never leave the house dressed like this."

Katie blushed. "Took a glass of wine." She diverted her eyes, suddenly shy? "OK, maybe two," she added.

When she looked back, the saucy vixen was back. "So, you know how *I know* you can't be my husband?" Her fingers tracing the make-up on my face. My hands drifted across her buttocks, where the pink bunny costume barely covered her. "My husband doesn't dance."

I just laughed, letting Katie guide me in the press of all those people.

We danced a few more songs before moving back to the bar for another drink. I ordered a soda, knowing that this night was nearing an end and Katie was in no shape to drive. I just wanted to fuck her.

"Looks like your husband's not coming out tonight," I said at the bar. She was sipping champagne, a drink that notoriously made her horny. And judging from the fire in her green irises, she was already plenty horny. "Want me to give you a ride home, Miss Bunny?"

"Gee, I don't know. Most people don't like to ride home with Death."

"I can take off my cloak if it'll make you feel better."

"Mmm, maybe not me, but I think I can make *you* feel better."

That sealed the deal. We were in such a rush to get outside that she didn't even finish her drink. I had to park a few blocks away, on a side street that was very deserted by the time we arrived.

"This your ride?" She ran her fingers along the sleek contour of my Mustang GT. "The Grim Reaper's a real American, I see."

Playboy bunnies and masculine cars... I thought, stopping short as she leaned back against the Mustang and stretched. Her bunny ears caught the light of a street lamp. I pinned her against the car and powered my lips into hers. It didn't feel like kissing my wife. It felt new and fresh.

I kept waiting for Katie to push me away, to suddenly regain her modesty. We were never big on PDAs and this was quickly headed to some pretty racy public displays. Instead, she thrust her chest forward, rubbing her body and breasts against me. This Playboy bunny was ready and willing.

My mouth and tongue ravished her neck, leaving her gasping into the chilly night air. With one hand still braced on the roof of my car, I dropped the right down along the pink satin of her dress and down between her legs. She parted her thighs a little, giving me access beneath the ultra short hemline. I felt the silk of her lingerie.

"Take off your panties," I urged, licking her ear.

"We shouldn't be doing this," Katie protested. I wasn't sure if the real Katie was back and she suddenly realized how public this was, or if she was continuing to play the game. I chose to interpret as the latter.

"Your husband will never know."

The brunette looked up and down the street. Seeing no one, she whispered, "I can't believe I'm doing this," before reaching under her dress and pulling down a pale pink g-string. She held it up, dangling from her finger. I could smell her arousal and see the damp spot on the front. "What now?"

"Put it in my pocket." She did so slowly, her lips curled up into the slightest of smiles. I felt her touch on my side, titillating my senses. She slipped her hand under the grim reaper robes, found my pocket, and stuffed them in.

I stepped forward, pinning her hand between us as we kissed again. This time, when my hand slithered between her legs, there was nothing between my fingers and her damp sex. But something was different. Where I expected to feel the softness of her curls along those familiar lips, I felt only smooth skin. Smoother than the rest of her body.

I pulled away, a little shocked at the revelation, and looked at Katie. Was this really my wife? Or some sexy impostor; a twin I'd never met, perhaps. The Katie I knew swore she'd never follow that trend, no matter how many times I'd suggested it.

She seemed amused by my reaction. She shrugged. "Goes with the Playboy theme, right?"

"God, I can't wait to fuck you." I buried my tongue down her throat and explored the newness of her cunt with my fingers. She'd left a little hair, I discovered, rising in a stripe above her hooded clit. Not quite a true Playboy model, apparently, but I wasn't about to complain.

"Turn around," I commanded.

"Max..." Katie balked.

"No one's looking. Do it." The look on her face was priceless. She was frightened, no doubt, but excitement was warring against her otherwise upstanding moral fiber. She touched the bunny ears as though reminding herself of the night and did what she was told.

I pushed open my robe and unzipped my pants, easing them down around my knees. Stepping close enough to pull the dress up to her waist, I let the robes fall back around us. At least we had a little modestly, I thought wryly, although no one was going to wonder what we were doing if they spotted us.

Cock in hand, I bent Katie a little lower over the car and entered her. Her nether lips swallowed me smoothly. It felt different, pushing inside of her without feeling the tickle of pubic hair. It felt strange and exciting.

"Bunny," I whispered when I sank ball-deep inside her. "I want you to imagine that I'm not your husband."

"Max..." she objected.

"Max isn't here," I corrected as I began to take her. Most of the time, I was a respectful lover. I paced myself, I matched her needs. We rarely just fucked like animals. Tonight, I was going to fuck her like an animal. "Imagine someone else. Do it, baby." I began jacking into her harder, using her cunt to get off. "Do it for me!"

I wasn't going to last much longer. Not after tonight. Not with this Playboy hottie between me and my Mustang. God, I never felt like such a man. Katie began to pant hard, her breath shuddering. She dropped her head down between her shoulders, bracing stiffly against the car.

Neither of us said a word other than sharing our ragged, passionate cries. Was she thinking about a stranger? A celebrity? Someone she knew and fantasized about?

The car rocked on its suspension as my pounding grew furious. Katie matched each stroke with a backwards shimmy of her own. When she reached behind me and placed a death grip on my hip, forcing me to fuck her faster, I lost it. She'd never done that before, not in eight years of marital fucking.

"Uhgod!" I groaned, all at once, and exploded inside of her.

Katie hissed, dropping her head even lower. She shoved backwards so hard we nearly ended up sprawled in the street.

I came and came, doing everything in my power to keep that guttural shout from clawing its way free. When it was over, I felt drained, my breathing hard yet not enough. I pulled away from Katie, who was once again my wife. We slumped to the asphalt, our sweat quickly cooling in the October air.

"Did you..." I couldn't quite come out and ask it: *did you really fantasize about another man?*

Katie looked worn-out, but in a sexy way. Her hairline was damp and her auburn locks were in disarray, but she was still more beautiful than most on their best days. She gave me a little nod, but that was all.

I collected her into my arms and together, we managed to get into the car. I barely remember the ride home. Both of us were still glowing from the excitingly new sexual experience, and I think both of us were afraid to talk about it.

By the time we got home, though, the reality of the whole night began to set in. The rational Max and Katie had returned to pay the sitter and kiss their daughter goodnight, and neither of them could believe they'd had sex on a public street outside a bar.

"Good night, Max," Katie said with an earnest look in her large eyes.

"Good night, Katie."

CHAPTER 4

Morning came with Mya calling out for Mommy. Normalcy forced its way back into our lives. *Grimm* and *Bunny* secreted back to wherever they'd come from.

"I'm never drinking again." Katie smothered her face with the pillow and groaned. For once, it wasn't me with the wicked hangover.

"That's a shame, because last night was a lot of fun."

Katie peeked out from beneath the pillow. "Oh, my God. I can't believe we did that."

"We didn't. Grim and Bunny did, remember?"

She ducked back beneath the pillow, a muffled, *Oh, my God,* just barely emerging.

"Mommy! Mommy, Mommy, Mommy!"

"I think you're being summoned," I said, running my hand up her naked back. I wished we had more time to fool around.

Katie dragged herself out of bed, forcing a smile. Morning light washed her nudity, glancing off the full swells of her breasts and the pale contour of her hips. I caught my first glimpse of her new hairstyle below. The dark red landing strip looked even better than it had felt, sitting like a coy reminder that she was a woman.

"That's so hot," I said.

Katie followed my eyes, her face growing red. "It hurt like crazy, so you better."

"You waxed?" I couldn't believe that the situation could get any hotter.

She pulled on a t-shirt and a pair of pajama pants. "Mmm hmm. I saw a deal for a Brazilian bikini wax on Groupon and decided to go for it. It was kind of weird, having someone else see me like that, but…I like the results."

She blushed again, raking her fingers through her red hair.

"Think you'll keep it up?"

"I'll think about it," she said.

"Mommy, Mommy, *Mom-my!*"

"Duty calls."

****

The time leading up to Thanksgiving was awesome for our sex life. We made love in the mornings before Katie had to go to work. We took advantage of the weekends like we hadn't before, and I made sure that I didn't have to cover anyone's shifts. I even put the business of the speakeasy on hold to focus on Katie and Mya.

We didn't mention my fantasy during that time—the sex we shared was sweet and intimate and free of any fantasies—but I could still feel it linger, like warmth in a bed just vacated.

When Katie had a week-long trip to New York, she asked if I wanted to join her at the tail end. "It's the week before Thanksgiving and I'll be free after Saturday. You can drop Mya at my parents' house and we can spend some time together, just the two of us, before driving up to them."

They lived in Connecticut, a long haul for us normally, and we'd planned on spending Thanksgiving with them.

A weekend alone with Katie in a strange city? Yes please. Maybe she'd come out of her shell a little bit more. Maybe we could try another role-play. It got me hot just thinking about the possibilities.

Of course, I didn't mention any of that to her. I had something good here, but it was delicate. Katie seemed interested in the fantasy beyond merely indulging me—*Bunny* made that crystal clear—but I didn't want to scare her off.

The evening before Katie was set to leave, I discovered just how delicate the fantasy was. I crawled into bed and asked her if she felt bad doing this behind her husband's back. My cock was already hard as the fantasy situation consumed me.

It was the wrong thing to say. "Max, can we just make love?"

"I'm sorry, it's just...I thought you—"

"It's our last time to be together until next weekend. I'd like my husband!" She laughed, but there was still an edge to it.

"I *am* your husband. I'm just trying to butter you up before you leave."

She shook her head slowly. "Butter me up? What makes you think I need any buttering up at all?"

And like that, my cock was as hard as a steel rod.

She rolled me onto my back and stripped out of her little booty shorts. Climbing over me, Katie made sure to run my member along her buttery smooth pussy lips. "I waxed this morning. Just for this trip," she whispered.

"God, I can tell." She was wet, too, her pink lips glistening beneath that auburn bar of pubes. "It looks great."

She shifted, placing me against her opening and sinking down. "I want to remember how good you feel, Max." She leaned forward, her lips finding mine as she pumped me slowly. Pulling back, she added, "Give me something to compare, baby."

I nearly lost it. She was actually playing the game. The electrical thought that she'd have a lover to compare me to nearly did me in.

Somehow, I managed to keep my balls from erupting. Somehow, I managed to regain control, palming her ass as she grinded into me. We didn't talk about it again, but I did as I was told: I gave her something to compare. I may have harbored a fantasy of her taking other lovers, but in the end, I wanted her to come home to me and acknowledge that they were all inferior.

I finished her off on top, her legs wrapped around my back and my balls clapping against her taut buttocks. We kissed until we couldn't. We bathed each other in our moans. And when I emptied myself deep inside her, I did it wondering if she ever would have someone to compare this with.

****

Katie flew out to New York the next day and was immediately caught up in meetings and work. I busied myself taking care of Mya, packing for our trip, and making sure that all the bars were ready for the Thanksgiving holidays. It was a tricky time of year since so many people took vacations, but unlike an office, we didn't have the option to close.

I flew into Connecticut Monday afternoon, dropped Mya off with Katie's parents, and politely declined their offer for dinner (they knew I would, else they wouldn't have offered). Instead, I grabbed some McDonald's at a rest stop on the way into New York.

Even on a Monday night, downtown Manhattan was a nightmare to drive through, and it was past 10:30 by the time I actually got to our hotel, parked, and checked in. I'd spoken with Katie a few hours ago, just after they'd wrapped up their session with their clients. They were going out to celebrate at The James, the speakeasy Katie had mentioned them visiting a few months ago. She wanted me to see how New York did it before we brought the idea back to our city, and I was all for it.

Changing out of my travel clothes and into some slacks and nice shirt, I caught a cab and arrived around 11:30. It was located in a shady part of Tribeca, and when the driver let me out in front of a nondescript building with no awning, no line, and no sign, I started to feel a bit sketched out.

Approaching the door, I noticed a small, brass plaque that simply read, "The James." No hours of operation. No "open" indicator. Not even a small, paneled window like what I'd seen in the movies. Uncertainly, I knocked and, much to my surprise, was greeted with a harsh buzzing like the door of an apartment complex. Pushing on the door, it opened to a set of descending stairs.

At the bottom, a tall, thin man wearing a crisp black suit met me. "Reservation?" he asked simply.

"Um, I'm meeting someone here. Katie Callahan?"

He gave a curt nod. "You must be Maxwell. Please, right this way." Going into this night, I wasn't sure what to expect from The James. As I stepped into the narrow speakeasy, I realized that this was exactly what I should have been expecting. It was dark and old feeling, trendy in an un-updated way. I'd been thoroughly transported into the Prohibition Era.

The bar's black shelves were stocked with a myriad of exotic liquors and a woman with unnaturally red hair was pouring some kind of milky white mixture into three martini glasses.

It was quieter than I'd expected, the soft din complimented by the lazy riffs of a muted trumpet. A few patrons were sitting at the bar, but most were spread out among the booths: polished black wood with red-velvet upholstered seats.

The host led me to Katie's group, whose table was littered with empty glasses. My wife smiled as she saw me approach, shouting, "Max, you're here!"

"Hey, honey." I leaned down and kissed her softly on the lips. She'd painted them bright red, which fit this place so well, and didn't want to smudge too much. "A cigarette, huh?"

Katie had a cigarette perched between her fingers. Back in college, she used to smoke when she drank, but I thought she'd given up on that habit.

Katie turned bright red. "Um, it goes well with absinthe."

"It's my fault, Max, sorry."

John stood, holding out his hand for a shake. John had become "Nadia's husband" in my brain. It was weird seeing him in my wife's world, even though that's how he'd met his future wife.

"No worries, John. It's good to see you."

"Likewise," he nodded. "I thought you can't smoke in bars in New York..."

Katie answered, even though my question was directed at John. "Unspoken agreement not to turn anyone in. It's part of the spirit of the speakeasy."

I took a seat, nodding at the rest of the group. The three other guys were in their thirties, and like Katie, were still in their suits. With their loosened ties and rolled up sleeves, I recognized their like from my shifts at the bar: they were the guys who'd let their happy hour extend too long.

I'd met them all before, but it had always been at some social event: a holiday party, someone's retirement. Other spouses had been present. Looking back at Katie in her unfamiliar dark suit and crisp blouse, I realized how weird this must be for her—two worlds colliding.

A server came around. I ordered a martini, figuring straight liquor fit the bill for this place, and toasted to the group. "To a successful whatever, may you have many more."

The mumbled response wasn't what I was expecting. Katie stubbed out her cigarette and gave a slight shake of the head: *We'll talk later,* that gesture suggested.

I wasn't here to rock the boat. When the morning came, Katie had to work with these guys. She had her work identity here: the mother hen in a group of raucous boys. She wasn't the oldest, but it was clear after the first half hour that she was the most mature.

As my second drink arrived, I realized how strong they were. I wasn't a heavy liquor drinker, but I didn't normally get buzzed after one drink. The McDonald's Value meal felt like ages ago.

"Hey, remind me not to make the drinks this strong when I open a speakeasy," I whispered to my wife.

"A Callahan speakeasy?" one of the guys asked, suddenly interested. "Back home?"

"That's the plan."

"Man, that's a great idea!" The others agreed, and I suddenly felt modest. "We need a relaxed place like this."

"It was actually Katie's idea." I wanted to put credit where credit was due. I patted her knee and smiled at her.

"You should go talk to the owner," John said. "I'm pretty sure that's her right over there."

The owner, it turned out, was the brightly dyed redhead working bar. She'd moved into a booth in the back of The James and was flipping through a three-ring binder of financials. I knew the feeling, although I usually did that in my office.

John introduced us, exchanging a European-style kiss on each cheek. *Pretty sure that's her?* I wondered, looking at him. He just shrugged and left us to chit-chat.

"I'm Tatyana." Her voice carried a light Eastern European accent. She was striking up close. The wrinkles around her eyes put her about my age, and the shock of fire engine red hair made her unblemished skin appear even paler. "It's so nice to meet another restaurateur. Or whatever we're called."

"Bar owner?" I offered. "Booze pusher."

"You're a funny one. Please, join me!"

It was the perfect solution to Katie and her two worlds. I could pass the time getting advice from the Tatyana, while Katie celebrated with her coworkers. The only drawback was that the drinks were free and I didn't have the heart to turn any of them down. By the time I made my way back to the accountants' table, I was trashed.

John had moved over to the seat I'd left and he and Katie were chatting away as the other three guys played quarters with The

James' expensive highball glasses. Definitely need to remember to make the drinks lighter, I reminded myself.

I paused a few booth-lengths away and watched my wife. The professional Katie and the home Katie weren't so different. In both worlds, she was a hard working, play-by-the-rules type of woman. She'd always been like that; that was the girl I'd fallen in love with in college. Work came first, then play.

But she also knew when to let her hair down—not literally, though. Tonight she'd arranged the copper locks into a tight, straight braid that hung between her shoulder blades. But as she spoke with John, another cigarette pinched between her fingers and a glass of some fancy gin drink in the other, she was relaxed in this element. She navigated it as well as I did the bar scene.

As I noticed John watching her, something else occurred to me—call it drunken intuition. He was into her.

I'd always thought of the quiet guy in one of two ways: he was either Katie's shy coworker, or Nadia's husband. He was never more complex than that—until now. Watching the two of them sitting so close, turned into one another, sent adrenaline racing through my veins. John talked; Katie was riveted. Was she into him, too? Impossible!

"Hey, guys." Both Katie and John jumped as I barreled back toward the table. The others just looked up from their game with amusement.

"Tatyana give you some good tips?" Katie put out the cigarette, even though it was only half-smoked.

"She did. But if I even catch another whiff of vodka, I think I'm liable to fall over."

"I thought you owned bars," one of the guys ribbed. I ignored him.

"Ready to head out, honey?" Katie asked.

"Oh yeah." *Just not ready to go to sleep.*

I offered Katie my hand even though I was pretty sure I was shakier than her. She took it, waving back at the table on her way out. "I'll see you guys after Thanksgiving."

I watched John carefully; watched that unmistakable look of longing. Even drunk, he kept it well concealed, but now that I knew what to look for, I knew that I saw envy there, too. It sent a thrill through my body, even as I thought of Nadia back home and how wrong this attraction was.

"God, I missed you, Max." Katie kissed me when we crawled into our cab. "I know my co-workers are sometimes a lot to handle."

"I don't know how you work with them sometimes. Seems like such a guy's world."

"Yeah, but I can hold my own." Good ol' boys or not, the group clearly respected her. "And John helps keep me sane." John. His name burned in my ears. "Anyway, I owe you for being a good husband." She kissed me softly on the cheek.

"Owe me what?" I reached out and stroked her leg.

"Mmm, a confession?"

Something tingled between my legs. "Oh yeah?"

"Mmm hmm." With that wide grin on her face, I realized she was drunker than I'd thought. Leaning close, she whispered, "I kissed a boy."

I was stunned. *Hello*. She had to be fucking with me? Another game. By now, she knew what turned me on.

I could feel the taxi driver watching us but ignored it. We were hundreds of miles from home, who was he to care? "When?"

Still smiling broadly, she replied, "Last month. Last time we were here."

"Why don't you show me how you kissed him." Katie bit her lip, making a nice show of being shy. "Pretend I'm that boy."

Taking a deep breath, she curled her hand behind my neck and drew me close. Our noses touched first. Then our lips. At first, I thought it would end there, lips on lips. She pulled me closer, tightening the innocent kiss.

Then she tilted her head and opened her mouth, prodding me with her tongue. I welcomed her slippery probe with my own as my cock lurched in my pants. She frenched me for a good 30 seconds more before pulling back, eyes averted, her lower lip tucked under a row of white teeth.

"Wow," was all I could say.

"You're getting off on this, aren't you?"

"It's crazy, but I am," I said. "Did anything happen after the kiss?"

Katie's green eyes blazed. "You wish something did?"

"I don't know..."

"What if I told you *yes*?"

"I'd ask you to tell me about it." I felt the exhilaration of hitting the peak of a rollercoaster—suddenly, the whole world dropped out beneath me. The cab rolled up in front of our hotel and the driver reluctantly asked us for the fare. He seemed as interested in this story as I was.

When I'd paid up, Katie slipped up next to me, arm in my arm. "This happened in the hotel bar, actually. Just around the corner. I asked him if he wanted to see the view from my room."

I could hardly breath. I knew it was a story, but the fact that she was really playing along was astonishing. Something out of a dream. We reached the elevators and I surreptitiously adjusted my hard on. "As soon as we were in the elevator, he was all over me."

Katie smiled as we stepped in ourselves.

"Show me."

My sexy wife wrapped her arms around my neck and pulled me close. This time, the kiss started hard and only got harder. The elevator doors chimed open before I wanted it to end. "Then you led him to your room?"

Katie nodded, taking me by the hand and guiding me down the hall. I lagged a little behind her, enough to check her out. She wore a dark suit, the kind with slacks that hugged her buttocks tightly before opening to a wide leg around her heels. Beneath the tailored suit jacket was a simple, silver blouse that buttoned up to a wide collar.

As soon as the door was shut behind us, I grabbed her from behind, reached around, and tore open the blouse. "What happened next?"

I pulled her braid and kissed along her neck.

"He was so excited. It was his birthday, you see, and he kept saying how this was the best birthday he'd ever had. So I asked him if he wanted to unwrap his present."

Christ, she was killing me. I turned her around and our mouths devoured one another. She met me with equal energy, her hands fumbling with my clothing as I tore hers off. Beneath the blouse was a lacy black bra. I left it on, along with the thong I discovered beneath her trousers.

"Did he unwrap you all the way?" I asked as she stepped out of her pants.

"No," she whispered, pushing me back onto the bed. She straddled me, rubbing her panty-clad pussy along my erection. I hadn't managed to get my own pants off. "No, he wanted me to do the last parts..."

Reaching behind her, she popped her bra off. Her full tits spilled forward, bouncing delightfully on her smooth body.

"Did he like what he saw?"

"Oh, yesss..." she gasped, grinding along my clothed cock. "You'd think he'd never seen a naked woman before."

"Probably not one as sexy as you."

"Jesus, Max, you're so hard!"

She slipped off me and sank between my legs, fishing me out. "Did you blow him?" My brain felt numb for asking, but not my body.

"Do you want me to have?" she toyed, wrapping her slender fingers around my shaft. She gave it a couple strokes.

"Yesss..."

With her eyes locked onto mine, she dipped her head down and took me into her mouth. Up and down she bobbed, warming up to the blowjob. I was fully erect, and Katie carefully eased it back into her throat. Watching those pretty red lips take me to the root— *no, take some younger guy to the root*—was practically enough for me.

"God, you're so hot," I groaned as she shifted between massaging me with her throat muscles, and corkscrewing up and down the upper portion of my shaft. Her fingers gently played with my balls, cupping and squeezing them as she worked. She must have felt them rise because before I even knew what was coming, she pulled back enough to catch the first spray of my come in her mouth.

"AH!" I growled, flopping back onto the bed and gripping the comforter hard. I thrust forward, feeding my spasming cock back down Katie's throat. She gagged a little before she recovered, and cum spilled down her chin, dripping onto her heaving tits.

She kept sucking until I had to push her away. It was too sensitive. "No more, no more!"

Amazing thing was that I was still hard.

Katie blinked at it, too, as she wiped her face clean with my boxers.

"That was... Jesus..." I was sweating and weak, my brain still buzzing. I managed to form a few words. "That was…"

"Good?" She stretched to full height. Katie hooked her thumbs into the sides of her thong and pulled it down.

"I think this is proof that it was good." I fisted my improbable erection.

"You're like my birthday boy." She positioned my cock against her pussy. "He didn't go soft after I sucked him, either."

"Really?"

Katie giggled some more. "No, not really! Fantasy, remember?"

"Yours or mine?"

She bent over me and kissed me softly. "Yours, darling."

"Based on how wet you are, I'd say it's partially yours, too."

Katie rolled her eyes. "Okay, maybe your fantasy turns me on a little." She bounced casually in my lap, lost in thought for a moment. "A couple months ago, I never would have thought of it. Then we had that talk. The night before I left for New York?"

"I remember."

"That night I was here, in this room by myself..." She hesitated a little, but didn't stop gently riding me. "Okay, I'll admit that I thought about it. A little. I couldn't help it. I wished you were there. To take care of me."

"I'm sure John wouldn't have minded." I hadn't intended it to be anything but a tease.

Katie stiffened on top of me, her eyes flickering down to mine quickly before she got control of herself. It was gone almost as quickly as it had arrived, but it left me feeling even more stunned.

"Why would you say that?" she asked, her tone controlled.

"Because he likes you. I saw the way he looked at you tonight."

Katie's laugh felt forced, but maybe that's just how I was reading it. "Why would John look twice at me when he's got Nadia at home. I mean, we're just friends, and—"

"Katie, Katie!" I reached up and pulled her down to me. I held her head against my shoulder and ran my fingers along the rippled texture of her braid. Even as I soothed her, my imagination was leaping to forbidden possibilities—possibilities that caused my heart to hammer and my gut to twist. Was something actually going on between the two of them? It was so out of left field that I didn't even feel jealous. I didn't know what to feel!

"I love you, Katie, baby. You're incredible. If you have anything to tell me, I'll understand."

She didn't do or say anything for the longest time. I could feel her heart close to mine. It was racing. At last, she snuggled closer to me, kissing my neck and chin. She nibbled down the line of my jaw and across my ear. "Max, I love you."

"I know." I prepared myself for a blow. I knew something was coming. I could hear it in the way Katie's breath caught. I felt it like a warm tingle along my fingertips and in every hair follicle.

She kissed across my cheek, stopping when our foreheads rested against one another and our eyes were inches apart. This close, neither of us would be able to hide a thing.

"Your fantasy scares me, Max. It's so wrong. So naughty. But I won't lie." She took a breath. "Since that first trip to New York, I haven't been able to get it out of my mind."

My gut tightened. "And?"

Katie's eyes shimmered. "And I really did kiss someone."

Bam.

All the saliva in my mouth dried up. I saw stars. I felt winded. And yet my cock surged inside of Katie's pussy: a towering demonstration of how fucked up my mind was.

"Just a kiss? Or…"

"Just a kiss."

I pressed. "Tongue?"

She leaned in and kissed me wetly. "Oh, yes."

"Why didn't you tell me?" I was close, and this time, when I released, I would be done for the night.

"I was afraid. Fantasy talk is one thing, but actually doing it… that's different."

"Are you still afraid?" I asked.

I could tell that she was, but like me, she was in love with the fear. "Yes."

"Me too."

She nodded, and that was that. The time to talk was over. Now, we needed to feel something base and raw. We needed to feel that love between us.

Katie rose back into a straddle, scooping up her breasts. They looked even larger in her little hands. Together, we began to grind against one another. I watched her smooth lips stretch and pull with each slow fuck. Pure skin-on-skin. I reached up and took charge of her tits.

Katie slid her fingers up to her face, her fingertips playing along her succulent lips. She closed her eyes, moaning with each entry.

We undulated faster. I squeezed the soft flesh in my hands, pinching her nipples harder and harder.

Stiffening above me, she cried out. Her braid whipped down across her back, the tip tickling my thighs. She thrust her breasts to the ceiling, shaking my hands free. I grabbed her waist, holding her upright as I felt myself letting go.

"God! Katie! FUCK!" I cried, releasing my come deep inside her.

"OH GOD!" she moaned, coming harder. Coming with me. "Max! MAX!"

"I love you, Katie," I croaked as she dropped heavily onto me body once again.

"I love you so much, Max. Thanks for…being you."

We had all these plans for the next few days: museums to see, restaurants to dine at. We ended up barely leaving the room. We fucked more than we did on our honeymoon. It was straight sex, no fantasies attached, but it was fantastic. I knew she had something on her mind. It took every ounce of willpower not to press it. She had to know I was thinking about it, too. We'd talk when she was ready, and for now, I was fine with that.

CHAPTER 5

The holiday season was always busy. This year seemed to be on a mission to outdo all the rest.

First, there was work. I came back from New York full of ideas on where to take my speakeasy and I could no longer hold back. I set a goal to pick a location before the end of the year, and on a lark, I looked into Chloe Reynolds' commercial real estate business. When I called her office (not her), I wasn't sure if I'd follow through with using them; I'd used a different company for all my previous bars. I was a little relieved when it turned out her group specialized in office space, not food and beverage. It removed the temptation to flirt with that dangerous road.

At home, our childcare situation became unsustainable. We'd been trying to make do without a nanny until Mya went into kindergarten, but she was still only four and it would be almost another year before that was possible. Katie working days and me working nights, on top of all the meetings associated with starting a new business, was spreading us thin. If we kept leaning on my parents to help out, they were liable to disown me by the New Year, so I made some calls and got her on the short list for pre-school starting after the winter break. That would help some. I could get my work done during the day and have my evenings free once again.

Which leads me to Katie and myself. In the weeks following our New York trip, I couldn't stop thinking about Katie's confession. Drunk or not, she'd kissed another man. Good Katie. Perfect Katie. If she was capable of that, maybe she was capable of more? The seed of doubt should have made me angry and upset; it should have forced me to confront her so we could work it out before there was any lasting damage to our marriage.

Instead, I got aroused every time. The simple thought that she'd given into her desire gave me a jolt that started at the tip of my little head.

It wasn't an easy thing to come to terms with. I obsessed over the speakeasy's design so that I didn't have to think about it all. I started working more and more from home so that I could watch Mya.

It didn't help when Katie came home, not even a week after New York, with worry etched all over her face. Throwing herself into a kitchen chair, eyes shut, she announced, "We're getting audited."

"We're getting what?!" As a business owner, this was probably one of my biggest nightmares. One bar getting audited was a pain in the ass. I owned three. I had my bookkeeping in order and nothing to hide, but there was just so much cash exchanging hands that things could get dodgy fast. "Why?"

Katie lifted her head. "Not you. Not the bars. The firm. My firm is getting audited."

A lot of things fell into place. Katie's stress levels. The somber mood at The James. All the trips back and forth to New York. Still, it didn't make much sense to me.

"Audited? Don't you guys do the auditing?"

Turns out, Katie's accounting and auditing firm was being investigated by the government. Her team was under pressure to produce clean books—something that was apparently harder for a multinational corporation to do than a chain of bars. The auditors were being audited. With billions of dollars being doled out by the American public, everyone was under scrutiny.

Her hours at work mounted. Katie's work life bled into her home life. She brought papers home, poured over the computer, made calls to international clients on behalf of people I didn't know.

Here's where I should have dialed back the fantasy, but I couldn't stop myself.

Katie had brought some paperwork home, explaining that they were going after her team. She was in the clear, but apparently none of the others were. "So you're speaking on behalf of John, huh?"

"Max, don't," Katie warned as I peered over her shoulder at her notes. The page she was on had all of John's accounts lined up. "I'm speaking for everyone."

"I just see John's name there," I continued. I even knew I shouldn't have been going there. I couldn't stop myself. "Should Nadia and I be concerned?"

"Not tonight, Max! Our jobs are at stake." Her eyes flashed as she glanced back at me, pulling her glasses off for emphasis.

That's where I should have ended it. If I were a smarter man, I would have. Instead, I said, "And what are you willing to do to save their jobs?"

"Jesus Christ, Max! What the hell's wrong with you!?" She pushed out of her chair and spun around to face me. "What do you want me to say? That I'll get on my knees and blow the auditors? That I'll sleep with a government regulator so they can look somewhere else?" She slumped a little, looking incredibly tired. "Please... not tonight..."

"Mommy, I can't sleep," Mya said sleepily from the doorway. "It's loud."

"Great, Max. Now I have to deal with this." She brushed by me before I could offer to do it for her.

****

Once upon a time, the thought of Katie's holiday party would have sent chills down my spine. Not only would she look fantastic (she always did, attracting the eyes of every straight male in attendance), but it would have given me more opportunity to observe her and John—something I hadn't been able to do since New York.

Unfortunately, the investigation had left the company morale in tatters. The government had come down hard on them, forcing many at the top to leave and the rest to restructure. Katie's team had escaped the worst of it, although it was dissolved and everyone reassigned.

The parties in the past had always been a little over-the-top. They'd rented out the party room at the Ritz, had an open (and very free flowing) bar, had a string quartet, and most people stayed well past midnight.

This year, the party was dry and the mood somber. Katie

looked fantastic in a long, red evening gown and her hair done up, and the men still looked, but even I was affected by the funeral-like feel of the night. John, Katie, and the rest of the team spoke quietly in a circle, wishing one another good luck on wherever they were going.

Nadia was there with John, of course, and the two of us ended up spending most of the evening talking to each other, a third-party to the tragedy.

Two of them had already taken offers from rival firms. Another had been "promoted" a management position in one of their smaller offices, managing local businesses. We still didn't know what was going to happen to Katie yet, but when I learned of John's fate from Nadia, I suddenly grew very afraid.

"He's going to New York?" I said. My mind was already making the obvious conclusions. I was about to lose my best employee—an employee that I'd begun to count on when I thought about opening my next bar.

"Yeah. We weighed the options together, but the New York position is a really good one. And the pay's unreal."

Nadia looked stunning, as ever. Her dress was black, short, and tight. Katie should have been overwhelmed by jealousy because of it; instead, Nadia's presence barely registered.

"When?"

"First week of the new year," she said.

"Fuuuck…" I ran my hand through my hair. "Were you going to give me notice?"

"What? Why would I…" She realized what conclusion I'd jumped to and shook her head. "Oh, no, I'm not moving with him. I'm staying here."

"You two are splitting up?" That was even worse.

"Wrong again. We talked at length about it. We both agreed that this was temporary, and that I shouldn't sacrifice my career for it. I'm going to need more weekends off, by the way."

"Long-distance? You?" I didn't mean to sound so skeptical, but the last person in the world I imagined could sustain a long-distance relationship was Nadia.

"Crazy, right? What can I say, I love the guy. This way, he'll be able to get his things in order, reach out to a few of the people he knows, and make a lot of money doing it. He's talking about starting his own business, even, so he may ask you for some tips."

"Wow. Change is in the air, isn't it?"

Nadia nodded. "You know what's not? Fun. Celebration. Drunken laughter."

I looked around at the mopey faces. "Some holiday party."

"I have an idea…"

At Nadia's suggestion, we moved the party to Callahan's, just down the street, and opened up the bar. We weren't able to salvage everything—the underlying sense of doom was never going to go away—but we did our best to get everyone stupid drunk.

I remember being slouched in a booth, somewhere around two in the morning, drunk off my ass and chatting with some guy I vaguely new from other such situations. He was slurring, I was close to it, and I wasn't sure I'd remember any of the conversations in the morning, but I'd already decided I was fine with that.

"I know we don't really know each other." The guy stabbed his index finger shakily at me. "But you're an okay guy."

"Thanks—"

"With an above okay wife, I might add. *And* an even more

above okay bar!"

"Oh-kay." I broke out into laughter, soon joined by the other guy.

"I don't know why I never came here more often. You're proud of it, I can tell." I nodded. It was my first—a symbol of all the risk I'd taken when stepping into this arena, and the faith that Katie had in me. "I like you. You're not afraid to share the things you love."

I happened to be looking across the room at my wife, who was chatting with one of the more senior members left present. His face was red from all the drinking, and his eyes couldn't stay out of the front of her dress. Katie seemed oblivious.

Not afraid to share the things you love.

It was true, and his statement hit me like a ton of bricks. I didn't remember anything else from that evening. If you asked me who I'd been talking to, I couldn't have told you. But that statement? That statement would stay with me for a very long time.

CHAPTER 6

Katie had made such a good impression when she'd defended her team that she was offered the newly created position of Director of Quality Assurance. It paid triple what she'd been making, came with a set of benefits that neither of us could believe, and was a huge promotion. Based on this promotion and John's, it seemed like her company believed that in order to save money, it needed to spend it.

The downside was that it involved a lot more travel than Katie's last position. She'd be visiting offices across the globe, including ones in London and Hong Kong.

"I don't know if it would be worth it," Katie fretted over dinner. "I'd be traveling… a *lot*. I don't want to miss these moments." Just five minutes ago, Mya had been chattering away excitedly as she gobbled down her food. Now, she was sound asleep, face down in her spaghetti and meatballs. It was adorable.

"True, but for everyone of these, there's The Supermarket Incident." A month ago, Mya had decided that she wanted this stuffed animal more than anything else in the world. When we told her she couldn't have it, the scene was not pretty. We literally had to drag her out the door, kicking and screaming. The experience had been mortifying.

"That's an excellent point! I'll call and accept right now!" Katie laughed. "Oh, Max, I don't know what to do."

"Try it," I offered, reaching out to touch her hand. "If it's a mistake, you can always quit."

It was the exact same advice she'd given me six years ago, when I decided to open my own bar. Without her push, I never would have tried it, and I wouldn't be in the process of opening my fifth.

Her face brightened. "I see what you did there." She laughed. "There might be times when I'm gone for a couple weeks at a time. What would we do about Mya?"

"I was thinking about moving my office here. And I guess it's time to look for a new nanny. Or at least a reliable babysitter."

"So you get all the cuteness time?" Katie looked lovingly at Mya. My wife got up and began gathering the sleeping girl for bed.

"And the supermarket time," I reminded.

"I love you, Max. Thanks."

"Hey, if this doesn't work, then at least you can say you tried it. No regrets."

"No regrets."

****

I had an uncle with a terrible drug habit. He died before he reached 50, bankrupt and strung out on heroin. He lost his job. His home. His wife and kids left him. And when he died in the hospital, he was alone.

The thing is, my uncle was a smart guy. He knew what he was doing, and what his addiction was doing to his life. On one of the few times I'd caught up with him sober, we'd had a long conversation about it. Drugs were bad, any idiot knew that. But they made him feel so good, and when the whole world was falling apart around him, at least he had that. He just couldn't stop. He had to have his next fix.

I used to wonder how a guy could ever get that low. I used to wonder how such an intelligent and successful man could lack any kind of self-control. But if I let myself reflect on my life up until now, I had to admit: I kind of did understand.

I consciously stayed away from any mention of my fantasy—at least with Katie. After her last outburst before the holiday party, when I'd teased her about John, I stayed mum on that subject. Instead, I fed the fantasy with a steady amount of Internet research. I learned that there was a whole subculture out there on the subject. I learned of terms like *cuckold* and *hotwife*. I lurked, not participating, but fascinated by what I found.

And that wasn't to say that our sex life suffered at all. If anything, it benefited from all the travel. It was a textbook case of absence making the heart grow fonder, and while it wasn't particularly imaginative sex, with a woman that looked like Katie riding you, who really cared?

I bonded with Mya a lot more now that I'd become her primary caregiver. I made sure that Katie wasn't too envious of her lost mommy time, making that she heard about every tantrum and blow up; how hard it was to put her to sleep at night; how she'd decided that she was never going to take her Shrek slippers off, even when going outside in the snow. Katie knew I was holding back, but appreciated it.

I compartmentalized the two visions of my wife: the good Katie—arguably the *real* Katie—and the one who kissed some stranger in New York and was turned on by my fantasy. It worked. For a good long time, it was fine. And then Katie dropped a temptation in my lap that I just couldn't resist.

"Hey, hon? Who's that real estate agent you use?" she asked as she bathed Mya before her bed time.

"What's that?" I asked. Katie was kneeling outside the tub, bent over enough that her jeans pulled tight across her ass and her turquoise thong was prominently displayed.

"Your realtor that you use for the bars. Who is it again?"

"Lee Heyman. Why, what's up?"

"Well, we need to relocate our office now that we've cut so much staff." She sloshed water across our daughter as she giggled away. "I got put in charge of the search committee for a new site. I thought of you and the speakeasy."

I still hadn't come up with a name, but even with a site picked out, we were a good six months out from opening.

"Well, Lee only handles food and beverage locations…" This was a light bulb moment, and once turned on, there was no way to turn it off. "If you're looking for office space, I have a few names."

Well, one name: Chloe Reynolds.

"Great!" Katie said, tossing me a smile over her shoulder. "Could you email me their contact info? I'll look into it tomorrow."

I emailed right after, before I lost my nerve.

I had a hard time sleeping after that. If I could have taken it back, I probably would have. I replayed the conversation again and again. Why hadn't I just said I didn't know anyone else? How was it that Chloe was still haunting me, nearly a year since I'd witnessed that game?

Yet it was out there and there was nothing more I could do but to wait and see what happened next. I secretly hoped that the Chloe lead was a dud, yet at the same time that Katie connected with the blonde.

When Katie came home and didn't mention a thing about the real estate search, I figured maybe she hadn't followed through on my recommendation. It made me part happy, part sad, but mostly relieved.

Ignore something for long enough, and it goes away, right? Wrong.

A week later, my action reared its ugly head. Katie had been in San Francisco for the week, but apparently she'd been busy on the phones. The day after she flew back in, she came home very excited. "That Chloe Reynolds is great! How do you know her again?"

I knew it was a loaded question. After all these years of marriage, I could pick out when she was testing me. I didn't want to lie and felt terrible for doing it, but I figured this was one of those situations where it was better to stretch the truth a bit.

"Actually, I don't know her. Her husband comes into Starlight every now and then."

"Well, she's good, I can tell you that. She had five different locations lined up with only a week's notice. God, I'm exhausted!" She fell into the sofa, still wearing her work clothes. "Heels were a mistake today."

"So?"

"I think we've narrowed it down to three sites. I'll let the committee vote on what they like better next week. Chloe said the market's slow, so we can be a little patient."

"That's great, honey." I hoped my smile was encouraging.

"Oh, and we're going out Friday night for drinks, so don't wait up."

I felt like a hornet had just landed on my sleeve. My first instinct was to swat it away. The more reasonable part of me counseled to stay quiet and let it fly away on its own.

"You and the realtor?" Was I blinking too much to be natural? "Chloe?"

OK, probably shouldn't have overacted so much. She picked up on it immediately; I was busted. "You've met her!"

"No. What?" I tried one last time to play dumb. Her eyes narrowed as she studied me. I scrambled before she put two-and-two together. "Okay, yeah, I've met her. She came into the bar with her husband once. I was just worried…you get jealous sometimes." Her face darkened and I went on swiftly. "So you two hit it off well, I take it?"

She held her stern face a moment longer. "She's great, yeah. I like her a lot. I can see why you'd think I might be jealous."

I balked. Katie burst out laughing, giving me a wink.

I tried to sound calm. "So where are you two going?"

Now it was Katie's turn to seem a little apprehensive. "Well, I mentioned that I like dancing. She said she knew this great salsa club…"

"Yeah?"

"Um, I could cancel. I mean, it's kind of weird, right? Going dancing at my age?"

"Are you kidding me? I think it's awesome."

Katie's worry lifted with a crooked smile. "Of course you'd think that. How could I forget?"

"I have no idea." I kissed her. "My only condition is that if anything happens, you tell me all about it."

"Nothing's going to happen."

"Right, but if something does…"

"Don't worry, Max. I know what you want."

****

I was so elated that my fantasy was back in play that I nearly forgot about the new player in the game. Chloe, the wild card. The next day, that wild card reared her pretty head.

My phone rang with a number that I didn't recognize. I considered just not answering. I let it ring three times before compulsion forced my hand.

"Hello?"

"Hey, Max." Chloe's throaty voice was unmistakable, even after all these months.

"Chloe." My face was on fire.

"I just picked up the most interesting new client last week. Pretty redhead? She shares your last name?"

"Katie. My wife. I gave her your number." If I kept putting my head in the sand, maybe I'd escape this one unscathed.

"Oh, I know. She told me you did. I found that interesting, too."

"Chloe…"

"She's really attractive, Max. Now I see why you weren't interested in going home with me."

My stomach rose up into my chest as I listened. My ears rang with shock. This woman was dangerous. Everything about her scared me. Yet I was riveted.

"You know, I think she and I could be great friends. Is that what you were thinking when you gave her my number? We'd become BFFs? I could introduce her to my lifestyle?"

"No."

"Liar." She laughed gleefully. I was totally busted.

"This was a mistake," I mumbled.

"Relax, Max. I'm just teasing. But that *is* kind of why you sent her to me, isn't it?"

I didn't answer. I couldn't. Saying *no* was pointless, and I didn't want to tell her that she was right.

"Want me to cancel our plans Friday night? Just say the word and something *will come up.*"

I couldn't hesitate anymore. The decision was back on me. I took a deep breath, shut my eyes, and answered. "No, don't cancel."

I could practically see Chloe's Cheshire cat grin. "I was hoping you'd say that. My husband's out of town, so I'm thinking that after we're tired of dancing, maybe I'd invite her and a couple guys back to our place…"

The lingering sentence detonated inside my brain. *Oh my God! Was this really happening?*

"I don't know if she'd go for that…"

"I'll play it by ear, but I think she'll surprise you." Chloe laughed a little more. "Did I mention she's really good looking. She into women?"

I gulped, having to adjust myself. "I wish…"

"Too bad," Chloe said. "I have to go. I'll call you Saturday, okay?"

My response was wooden, like the way I felt. "Sure."

"And Max? Do me a favor; don't have sex with her before that night. I want her really worked up."

Jesus fuck…

****

Watching Katie get ready Friday night was one of the hottest experiences of my life. I'd been unable to concentrate on a single thing all day long, and as the sun set, my excitement and anxiety levels rose.

"Are you sure this isn't too short?" Katie appraised herself in the full length mirror one more time.

The honest answer was *yes*. But I wasn't going to answer that way. I dutifully assured her that the tight red number was fine for a night of dancing. Even with the ruffled flounce of the dress, designed to bounce and sway around her legs as she spun, it would have been considered short. Instead, I said, "You need to be able to move, right?"

"That's true..."

Truth and white lies. I'd been mixing them up so much lately. Like Chloe and this set-up. The guilt ate at me. I needed to tell Katie. I needed to confess. This wasn't me telling her that the grocery store was out of organic milk when really I'd forgotten to buy some. This little fib could lead to Katie crossing a line that would change us forever. And yet...

"How about these shoes?" Katie turned on her blood red heels, tall and strappy. Her legs shined with lotion.

"Amazing," was all I could say. The confession would wait a

day longer.

I watched her move. I loved how full her breasts looked in haltered outfits, and I'm sure all the men at the club would, too.

She went to put on make-up. I said, "Katie, I want you to have fun tonight. Promise me, okay?"

She gave me a questioning look in the mirror. "Okay."

I'd done as Chloe had ordered, despite all reason. Katie and I hadn't slept with each other since the phone conversation. It hadn't been hard to arrange. Sex was something we had to force into our busy schedules, not the other way around. I had to feign tiredness when she came on to me late last night; she said she was all worked up over the dress she'd purchased for dancing. Resisting her soft body had been incredibly difficult, and as I watched her put that dress on, I wondered if I'd made a huge mistake.

"I know things have been tough for us. You've been traveling, and Mya's been wearing me out...I just want you to know that if you wanted to cut loose tonight, I'm okay with that. You deserve it..."

Katie set her mascara brush down, reading between the lines of my stumbling admission. It had been a while since I'd brought up The Fantasy, as I'd started to think of it. I'd been careful not to turn her off to it. Now, seemed like the time to bring it up again.

"Max, I'm just going dancing."

I slid into the seat behind her, wrapping her up in my arms as I held her eyes in the reflection. "I know that, but there will be guys there, right?"

"Yes, of course."

"And you'll probably dance with a few of them, right?" She nodded. I continued. "And this time, the good ones probably won't be gay..."

"Max, if you're being jealous—"

"I'm not jealous." I slid forward a little more on our shared seat, my erection poking into her butt. I was hard as a brick; there was no way she'd miss it. "Just promise me you'll have fun, okay? And don't think about me."

She wiggled her hips against my erection. "Now it's going to be hard to think about anything *but* you. I wish we had a little more time."

I retreated from the seat before things heated up even more. Adjusting myself, I flopped back on the bed. "But we don't. You'll have to work your energy out at the club. With some strangers."

I bounced my eyebrows at her. Katie just rolled her eyes.

As we kissed goodbye at the front door, I whispered, "Seriously, let loose, honey. I trust you. My only request is that if something *does* happen, that you tell me all about it when you get home."

"Maxwell Callahan, *nothing* is going to happen!"

****

The night crawled by, each hour stretching hesitantly into the next. I felt the proverbial pins and needles assault my skin. My stomach couldn't settle. I couldn't sit still.

Things were better before Mya went to sleep. I had her to distract me. I had responsibilities. But when she was asleep and the house was dark and quiet, my insecurities slouched out of the shadows.

Was she having fun? Did she catch the eye of any one guy in particular? Was Chloe encouraging her? Had they already retired back to the blonde's house? What was this going to do to our marriage?

Was this all some huge mistake?

I had my phone at my side, clutched in a sweat-damp hand and ready to answer at a moment's notice. But it didn't make a sound until a quarter to two in the morning. It chirped, a text coming in.

–Getting coffee with Chloe. Be home soon.

The first thing that came to mind was the totally innocuous observation that Katie never used abbreviated grammar, even in texts. The second was a burst of anxiety. It felt like a bucket of scalding water had been dumped down my throat and was on its way to burning the inside of my stomach. Was she really just getting coffee? Kind of late for that...

I'd staked out on the living room couch, at first determined to be awake when she got home. When she'd texted me, I'd been dozing. After reading it, I was wide awake again, but that didn't last. My eyelids drooped. How I could be tired was beyond me. Jittery yet exhausted, I felt like I'd had too much caffeine and too little sleep.

I woke to the soft sound of the front door opening and closing. In the darkness, with my eyes still adjusting, I couldn't see the time other than that it was past 2. I blinked sleep away.

Katie was leaning on the inside of the door, breathing deeply, eyes closed. When I said, "Hey there," she jumped. Her eyes popped open, zeroing in on me.

"You're still awake." Her voice sounded hoarse.

"Not really." I sat up on the couch and rubbed the sleep from my eyes. It was nearly 3 in the morning. "You have fun?"

Katie nodded. I watched her cross along the floor, a little wobbly on her legs. She tossed her purse onto the armchair and lowered into my lap. Her hair, which had been so perfectly coifed when she'd left, had begun to unravel. It looked sexy.

"You smell like smoke," I said as she wrapped her arms around my head and kissed me softly on the lips. She tasted like smoke, too.

"I may have had a cigarette or two," she giggled huskily. Beneath the acrid tinge of the cigarettes, I could smell vodka.

"So whatever happened to leaving at 2?"

"I wasn't ready to come home. When the club closed, Chloe suggested this place around the corner where we could come down from all the dancing, you know?"

"So the club got you worked up?"

"God, yes!" Katie's laugh was so genuine and pure, yet it somehow sent such dirty thoughts to by brain. "Salsa is *so* sexy!"

"Meet anyone special?"

Katie's hesitation said as much as a confession. My throbbing cock reacted like it was.

"There was a guy," she said at last.

I pulled her body a little harder into my lap. Her hip rubbed along my groin, where I made sure she felt the stiffness of my cock.

Amazingly, Katie looked surprised. "You're really not mad?"

"Does this feel like I'm mad?" I could feel her hot skin beneath the thin material of her dress.

"Not any kind of mad I know of," she giggled.

"So...talk...tell me about tonight. Tell me about this guy?"

"Okay," she said at last, standing up long enough so that she could reach under her dress and pull off her thong. "But I need you inside of me. Right now."

After denying both her and me all week long, I was only too happy to oblige. With practiced efficiency, Katie yanked my pajama pants down, took hold of my cock, and straddled my lap. The short dress shielded our union, heightening the buttery smooth sensation of her pussy around my girth.

"I'm not the only one turned on," I groaned. She was almost as wet as she was after I'd spent myself inside of her. My heart skipped a beat as a thought pierced the veil of my lust. "Am I the first one in here tonight?"

Katie slapped me lightly on the shoulder as she dragged me into her cleavage. "You're a pervert, Max. You're the only cock I need."

I almost said, *We're not talking about need,* but held my tongue. "So this guy…was he good looking?"

She moaned softly, riding me in silence for a few minutes. I began to wonder if she was done talking for the night—that the booze and the late evening were finally catching up.

"The salsa club was packed when we got there. Full of really great dancers." She undulated a few times, remembering. "I mean, it was a true Latin night club. Chloe and I were one of the few white girls there."

"You're a great dancer," I interjected.

"I know, silly! I'm just telling you…so you get the idea. Latin dancing…"

"And Latin men," I finished for her, catching on.

"Exactly. The kind of men who don't take no for an answer."

"That what happened with this guy?"

Her pussy walls rippled around me as I mentioned him. God, her body felt good, alive and warm against me.

"I'll get to that in a sec. So when we got there, we were instantly approached by guys. Buying us drinks, wanting to dance with us." She laughed lightly. "It was like going from zero to sixty in ten seconds. Before I knew it, I was doing shots with a bunch of guys before being whisked back onto the club's floor."

She paused, savoring the feeling of my manhood slicing into her. "God, you feel so good," she whispered. "So most of the guys were jerks. I know I'm supposed to like bad boys, right? But I really don't. Then, we met Julio and Marcus."

"They were gentlemen?"

Katie burst out laughing. "No way! But they were *great* dancers. They were also incredibly hot." Now it was my turn to react inside her. I'd never heard my wife call anyone *hot* before. I didn't know how to explain it. It's not that I wasn't jealous—my blood was boiling with jealousy—but it was such a turn-on, too.

"You told me to let loose, so I kinda did." Her hair fell across her eyes. She pushed them away and glanced down at me. "I'm going to be a wreck tomorrow. Jesus, I can practically see two of you!"

"Well, when I said let loose, I didn't mean drink enough vodka to fill Lake Michigan!" I teased.

Katie giggled, but her eyes suddenly got a little serious. "Max, I..." She hesitated. I held my breath. "I love you," she finished.

God damn it, that wasn't what she was about to say!

"Turn around," I ordered, pulling up on her hips. Katie did as she was told, my cock losing contact with her pussy only long enough for her to swivel around and lower back onto it. Facing away from me, maybe it would be easier for her to talk.

"So," I began, cupping her full and unfettered breasts in my hands, "which one did you dance with most?"

"Julio," my wife said, her voice barely audible.

"Did Julio get to touch these?"

"He... yesss..."

My cock lurched inside of her. Jesus! Another man fondled my sweet Katie's tits! "You let him?"

"Not at first," she tried to console. "I mean, at first, I thought he was doing it, you know, by accident. Or something."

"Mmm, or something..." I agreed. "Did you kiss him?"

Her body shuddered as a miniature orgasm flashed through her body. "Uh, God..." she moaned, leaning forward and driving her hips into my lap.

"I'll take that as a yes," I chuckled. Christ, how could I be so fucking calm? "More than once?"

"Max, I—"

"More than once?" I cut her off.

"Uh, huh," she confessed.

I pushed her dress up around her waist so I could gaze at the heart-shaped perfection of her buttocks. They shivered with each backward slap of our skin on skin. "Did you two do anything else you want to confess?"

Once again, I found myself holding my breath. When she recovered from her orgasm and shook her head, I let it out. Disappointed.

Disappointed?!

Then she dropped the bomb.

"Julio wanted...he wanted to fuck me." She forced the words out. Hips in hand, I began to direct the force of our fucking, taking her faster and faster. I wasn't going to be able to hold out much longer. "I told him I was married, but he didn't seem to care. He offered to show me how a *real man* did it."

"Oh yeah?" I said. I reached forward and clutched her shoulder, yanking her body upright. She squealed a little. My cock realigned inside her pussy, each thrust driving harder against her g-spot. I knew she loved this position, and I knew that right now, she wanted it a little rough.

"I knew you'd be mad," Katie whined, teetering on the edge of a much bigger orgasm than the one previous.

"I'm not mad," I grunted, snapping the halter top and pulling the red material away from her bouncing tits. Grabbing them, I found her hard nipples and twisted.

"AH!" she cried out before she could stop. She bit down on her lower lip, the subsequent moans muffled in her throat.

"I just want you to remember how this *real man* does it."

She stretched back against me, pushing her tits into my hands as her hips grinded in my lap. "God, baby, I love you! Fuck me, my real man! Fuck me! Fuck me!" Her quiet cries punctuated each roll of her pelvis.

"Katie," I whispered, nibbling on her ear. "You were curious, right? About what it would be like to fuck him?"

She didn't answer verbally. She didn't need to. She went off like a bomb, shoving her head back over my shoulder as her cunt shuddered around me. She had. She was thinking about it. Right now! She was thinking about Julio's cock in her pussy. Julio's hands on her tits.

I came with her, firing the pent up lust deep into her. I pulled her close as I shuddered, squeezing the softness of her breasts. Our bodies shivered and spasmed.

"Are you telling me the truth? Or teasing me?" My throat felt raw.

"In this case, is there a difference?" She kissed my chin gently. "You wanted the truth, right? Yes, I made out with another man tonight. And yes, he told me he wanted to fuck me."

"And you wished you'd said yes?"

"Sweetheart, I told you, I don't need anyone else but you."

"You know that I'd be okay if you had said yes, though, right?" I held my breath as I waited for an answer.

Katie twisted in my lap, her face glistening with perspiration. "Oh yeah, your reaction made that pretty clear. But seriously, you're the only man for me. We're just having fun."

****

Impressively, Katie was downstairs by 9, dressed and ready to hit the farmer's market with Mya and me. "Good morning, Kates. Didn't expect you up for another couple hours."

"And miss this time with you guys? Forget it."

As we stepped out into the cold, the three of us holding hands on the short walk to the outdoor market, it was hard to believe that the woman at my side was the same one who'd come home to me last night. As she and Mya browsed the root vegetables offered by our local farms, I tried to get my head around it. She was Katie again, wearing a pair of jeans, her white tennis shoes, wool pea coat, and knit hat. Her ponytail escaped the hat, the cold winter sun turning it into shimmering copper. She pulled a couple sweet potatoes out of the pile and placed them on her head, like the horns of a bull, then pretended to gouge the giggling Mya.

That same woman had hooked up with another guy last night? It didn't feel real. I couldn't unify the two.

We went to the park after the market, even though it was cold enough to snow and we were the only family crazy enough to be out here when we didn't have to. Katie and I stood along the perimeter as Mya ducked and dove through the freezing jungle gym like it was the height of summer.

Katie was quiet, standing a couple paces away, watching Mya. She wore a smile, but it looked forced. I sidled up to her, pulling her gloved hand into mine.

"Thinking about last night?" I asked.

Katie shook her head. "I'm thinking about this. What we have right here. I don't want to lose this."

"You won't."

"Last night—"

"You had fun. I told you to let loose, and I'm glad you did. You need it."

Katie snorted. "I only need you, Max."

"Okay." I snuggled closer, taking a different tactic. "Then you *wanted* it. You've been under a lot of stress. Last night was just a way of relieving some of it."

"I can *relieve* it with you just fine," she said.

Our breath plumed in soft cloud that mixed before disappearing into the cold air.

"Come on, don't deny that you didn't have fun last night. I had pretty solid evidence last night that you did."

Katie giggled. "Yeah, that's kind of the problem. I think I had too much fun. I made out with another man."

I would never grow tired of hearing her confess to that. My cock was awake. My ears were open.

"And you liked it. It's okay, Katie. I'm okay with it."

"Explain that to me," she said—the same words I'd used on Chloe's husband over a year ago.

"You love me, right?"

She squeezed me against her. "Of course."

"Would you ever leave me?" I asked. Before she could reply with the obvious answer, I pressed on. "Last night, did it even cross your mind that you'd leave this," I swept my hand across the vacant playground, "for him?"

"Not once. How could you even ask that?" Katie said.

"I know you wouldn't. I know the answer to those questions. But I'm making a point. I'm not worried about *us*—about *you* and *me*. What we have is stronger than anything a kiss can undermine. Or even…more…" I petered off, but we both knew where I was going.

"You'd be okay with that? Seriously?"

"Seriously. As long as you were honest with me." I took a deep breath. This was the core of my fantasy—the one that I didn't fully understand, but was so intimately familiar with now. "Last night, did he really tell you he wanted to sleep with you?"

"No. He told me he wanted to *fuck* me," Katie said playfully.

"It makes me crazy hot even thinking that he said that to you, you know that? And…you could have said yes. Like I said, my only request is that you tell me about it. I need to know. That's how this works."

"I'll keep that in mind." She squeezed my hand, and that was that. "So tell me about something else. How's the speakeasy going? Do you have a name yet?"

I had the inkling of one, but I was still working it out in my head. It wasn't ready for primetime yet. "Going pretty well. I've got the lease signed, although it doesn't start until March. I'm hoping for a summer opening because those are always the best, but you know how contractors are."

"Twice as long and twice as expensive," she said. "Summer would be good, though. Anything I can do to help?"

Mya was storming down the twisty slide, laughing as she tumbled along the ground.

I said, "Help me find a nanny that can keep up with her? If you're still traveling this spring and summer, I'm going to need some help."

"That, I can do."

****

Monday, Chloe called me. I recognized the number, even if I hadn't programmed her name into my phone—my way of pretending that I hadn't really set Katie up.

"Hello?"

"Hello, Max." I'd secretly held out hope that I'd remembered the number wrong. I hadn't. "Sorry I didn't call Saturday like I said. Hope you weren't going crazy for an update."

Truth was, I had forgotten all about her promise. I didn't tell Chloe that, though. She struck me as the type who liked others anticipating her.

"I got one from Katie, actually. Sounds like you and her had a good time."

"We had a great time. She's awesome. I haven't had that much fun in a while. She's smart, a good dancer, is crazy attractive… she reminds me of me, actually." Chloe laughed. "Maybe me a few years ago, anyway. If you could have seen her, you would have been proud. You should have seen the guys flocking to her…well, the two of us. They were practically falling over each other to get the next dance. My feet are still sore, actually. Heels are evil."

"She told me about the guy she danced with a lot. Julio?"

"Mmm, Julio. Yeah, he was hot," Chloe said. The confirmation that he was real was like a vice around my chest. "I was kind of jealous."

Ditto to that.

I didn't want to ask my next question, but I couldn't *not*. "Did anything happen?"

"Well, I mean, it was salsa, you know? Sweaty bodies twisting and rubbing in the dark is what it's all about." My breath caught as her words came to life in my mind. "And there was definitely a period where I lost track of them on the dance floor. I asked her about it after we left the club. She said they stepped outside to have a cigarette and ended up *all over each other.*"

"Really?" I felt like the air had just been sucked out of me. "Did she tell you anything else?"

"She said he was too pushy. He wanted her to leave with him, even after she told him that wasn't happening. We actually ended up talking about you after we left. We got into some of your fantasies of her and other men—"

"You—"

"Relax, I played dumb. We connected over it. I told her all about my husband and his kinks. She seemed really interested in that, by the way. That we actually did that kind of thing. I told her that it wasn't right for every couple, but if you can make it work, it's incredible."

"Did it shock her?" I asked quickly, imagining Chloe confessing *that* to my wife.

"You'd think so, right? But it didn't as much as I'd expected. She seemed...intrigued. I don't think she'd ever thought about it from her perspective—as her own fantasy, you know? She told me she'd always thought it was some scheme of yours to get with another woman—"

"That's not it at all!"

"Calm down, honey. I know that...although you have to admit, you've thought about it."

"I haven't—"

"In any case, I think she's finally looking at it as something for her—not just you." Her voice got a little lower when she added, "She asked me if I loved my husband—which I do. She asked me if he knew about the other men. I told her he knew about most of them—she seemed interested in that, by the way. I could see it on her face. She didn't follow up, though.

"She asked if my husband was really into it, and I told her of course. I told her to tell you all about what happened, to gage your reaction. You can thank me for Friday night, now."

"Um...thanks." It felt like I was admitting to something illicit. I was.

"I think you, me, Katie, and my husband should get together for dinner. I think we have a lot in common."

I licked my lips, feeling heat sizzle along my nerves. That was dangerous. Anything could slip out...like the whole truth.

"I don't know."

"You want to take this further?"

I barely trusted myself to speak. "Yes."

"Then you're going to have to let us help..."

CHAPTER 7

"How did you meet Chloe again?" The question came a week later. She'd just come back from a short trip to New York and I made sure not to work that evening.

Her question sent a lick of heat across my scalp. I scrambled to remember the little white lie I'd already told her. "They've been into Starlight a few times."

"Together? Or..."

"No, not together."

Her eyes narrowed, but at least she smiled. "There something you left out when you recommended Chloe to me?"

Katie was too smart not to be suspicious. I could either dig myself deeper, or come clean. I decided to come clean.

"So I may have met them a while back."

Katie's face darkened. I hurried on.

"I actually did meet her husband first. He was at Starlight...you know, I don't think I even know his name?"

"Greg," Katie said flatly.

"OK, so Greg was sitting there, alone at the bar when Chloe came in. They acted like they didn't know each other, but I later found out that they did. Chloe flirted with some guys, let herself get picked up, and left with the guy. After that, I talked a little to...Greg. At the time, I thought it was totally bizarre...like, weird, you know?"

"And now you don't think it was."

Now I didn't. Was that true? I said, "I guess not. I mean, it's not totally normal behavior, but what's normal?"

Katie took a seat at the table, folding her arms under her breasts. "So that was it? You saw them once, then happened to have Chloe's number when I needed a realtor?"

I was treading dangerous water here. I could feel the heat of her anger and jealousy. How was I going to get out of this one? I tried the truth. "The next time I saw them was months later. Actually, this time it was just Chloe. We got to talking, and..." Katie raised an eyebrow. I hurried on. "And I ended up talking to her about you. And us. She recommended trying a role-play—"

"Was this around the time I went to New York?"

I hedged. "Maybe."

"And Halloween?" she asked. "Have you seen her since?" Her voice cracked like a whip.

"No, I haven't." Talking to her on the phone wasn't seeing her, I reasoned, although I made the split second decision to stop doing even that. "I swear to you, Katie, there's nothing going on between us. I understand why you might feel threatened, what with her lifestyle and all, but you have to trust me."

Katie's face finally softened, and as it did, she suddenly looked exhausted. "I trust you, honey. I just get—"

"Jealous. I know."

Katie's next question was expected, but no easier to answer. "Do you wish I was more like her?"

"I love *you*. The way you are."

Katie rolled her eyes. "Canned response. Be real with me, Max."

This question had no correct answer, so I asked it back. "Do you?"

She was smart enough to see what I did and could have turned it back on me. But we were getting nowhere, so she volunteered to take the first bold step. She took a deep breath. "Yeah, sometimes I do. I'll admit that a year ago, I would have thought you were crazy to suggest...other men. Maybe you've worn me down. I don't know, but..."

Her face flushed. She hesitated, looking up at me.

"What?" I asked.

"But I think about it a lot. Like, all the time."

"Really?" Then, because I wasn't sure I was following: "Think about what?"

"Other guys. Not seriously or anything, but... So when I go to the grocery store, I find myself sizing guys up. What would it be like to kiss the young cashier? Or the guy restocking the melons. I think about it at work, when I'm in meetings. I go around the boardroom, prioritizing the men from most desirable to least."

"No way." This was crazy talk.

Katie's eyes fluttered away from mine, but ended up steadying. "It's terrible. I'm like a...like a guy."

I laughed. "Pretty much."

"And then that thing in New York happened. I went too far. I freaked out. I could easily have taken him upstairs. Part of me *wanted* to."

"Part of you regrets not doing it?" I asked.

She exhaled loudly. "Geez, I don't know. No, I don't think so. I mean, you may have been okay with that, but I wouldn't have. Not at the time..."

My blood pressure soared. "Not at the time?"

She ignored the question. "And then last week, at the club..."

"You just kissed, right? Did anything else happen?"

She leveled a look at me. "Yes, just kissing. Ha. Since when did kissing another man seem so innocent?"

"Oh don't worry, I don't think it's innocent at all."

"You know what I mean." We stared across the table for the longest time. "You know, Chloe asked if we wanted to get together with her and her husband."

"*Get together* with them?"

"For dinner!" She paused, adding, "I think."

We laughed.

This felt more correct. More balanced. I'd been pushing us along this path, but for it to work, it needed to be a joint decision.

"What do you think?" I prompted.

She watched her own fingers twist and wring. When she answered, she didn't immediately meet my eyes at first. "I think it could be fun."

"Then why don't you set it up."

"Just dinner."

"Right. Just dinner."

****

We ended up not being able to set up the double date for an-other two weeks due to our schedules. We settled on Manchego, a hip new tapas restaurant that was about as expensive as it was exclusive. Friday reservations required a few weeks advanced no-tice—unless you had connections. I didn't make the reservation (and even by pulling the strings that I had, I wasn't sure I could), so either Chloe or Greg were hooked up.

The restaurant was located in the midst of a row of new and upscale restaurants downtown. I'd considered this area for the speakeasy, but the rent was too high for the type of crowd I was expecting, so I'd passed. The interior was cozier than I'd expected; so often, trendy hipster restaurants felt cold to me. This little tapas spot was very inviting.

We arrived first, so headed for the bar, hand-in-hand.

"I think I could use a drink," I said, squeezing Katie's hand.

"Nervous?" She asked the question, but she was feeling the anxious buzz, too.

"I feel like I'm on a first date or something."

"Me, too," she said.

I ordered a vodka martini and a margarita for Katie. The bar, like the intimate tables throughout the narrow space, was made up of Spanish tile. A nice touch, I thought absently, my eyes on the door.

"You look nice," Katie said, touching my tie and drawing me back to her.

I'd picked my outfit with the care of a first date, too. When I heard the name Manchego, I knew this would be more than a casual outing, so I went with my black Armani and a tailored shirt—pow-der blue with white French cuffs. The suit fit my slender frame well.

I was more a t-shirt and jeans kind of guy, but knew how to clean up when I needed to.

"You don't dress up this nicely for me anymore. I'm jealous," she pouted.

"I could say the same about you..."

The black dress wasn't as small as the LBD that Chloe had worn the first time I'd met her, but it was pretty damn small. Long-sleeved and wrapped around in front, it offered a tantalizing amount of cleavage—more so than Katie had ever been comfortable with before. In the past, she would have put a tank top or t-shirt on beneath to cover her chest—tonight, I swear she must have gone with a push-up bra.

Katie crossed her long legs on the stool, drawing my eyes. Black stockings encased them and I was pretty sure they weren't pantyhose.

"Got to make a good first impression," she said. Our drinks arrived.

"To new adventures," I toasted.

"Max, what are we doing here?" The question wasn't a veiled way of suggesting we leave, so I took it at face value.

"We're just going to have a conversation. Think of it as information gathering."

Katie nodded, wanting to believe it. "I know. It's just that this feels so...wrong. We're parents! How can we be doing this? What would my mother think if she knew?"

"But she doesn't," I reminded her. "And she won't. Besides, we're just talking, right?"

"Right. Just talking."

Greg and Chloe arrived before we reached the bottom of our

drinks, but only just. Chloe looked as ravishing as ever in her strapless black dress, but I made sure not to linger on her. This evening would go south in a hurry if Katie felt threatened. So instead, I fell into conversation with Greg.

My initial impression of him, formed so long ago, was of a passive guy, drawn through life by his firecracker wife. I still remember him hunched over his drink as Chloe flirted in front of him. Now I understood what he was going through; understood the emotional lash that you couldn't get enough of.

The man who shook my hand at Manchego was totally different. He still looked the same—same curly hair, same good looks just a shy too boyish to be considered handsome—but the demeanor was all wrong. His grip was strong. His blue eyes met mine without apology.

"Nice to meet you, Max," he said. I wasn't sure if he didn't remember me, or if he was just covering for the lie that I'd already confessed to Katie. It didn't really matter, though.

"Greg." I returned the shake.

"And you must be Katie. Very nice to meet you," Greg said. He didn't leer at her. He kept his eyes up as he took her hand and shook it.

I almost laughed at the formality of it all. Not that anything was going to happen tonight, but these were known swingers, and here we were, introducing each other like we were at the neighborhood block party.

"Chloe tells me you're an accountant?"

"I am. Exciting, huh?"

"I don't think it isn't. We move in the same circles. I'm a financier."

Katie laughed. "You mean you're a rich playboy?"

Greg joined her laughter. "I like to think I help others achieve their dreams, but sure, you could call me that."

Chloe interrupted. "Come on, our table's ready."

We ended up sitting around a small table in the corner, alternating male-female. Katie was on my right, Chloe was on my left.

How strange was it to be sitting across the table from the guy who'd planted the seed of my now fully matured fantasy? How do you start a conversation with a guy like that? *So my wife and I were considering bringing other men into our bedroom...could you pass the roasted cauliflower please?*

Katie started us off with more innocuous chatter. "So a financier? Did you finance any companies I may have heard of?"

"Probably not. Most of my investments are in small tech companies. High risk, high upside sort of things." Greg rattled off a list of names that I'd never heard of. Katie stopped him on the last.

"Nimbus Solutions? The video streaming company?" Katie asked. Greg nodded. "Our firm works with them. We perform their annual audit. Nice bunch of people."

"Yeah, that one was a no brainer. Sometimes, you can just tell by the quality of the people working there. Mostly what I do is read the people and the culture. If that's off, then I don't invest."

"You should have read the culture where I work." She delivered it through a row of pretty, yet gritting, teeth. She was still bitter from the IRS audit and all the scandal that went down—bitter at the dissolution of her team.

"Which firm?"

When she told him, his eyes went up. "I read about that in the news. Tough times."

"Oh, yeah."

The server came along just as I started feeling totally shut out of the conversation. We ordered a number of small dishes to share (I didn't miss the irony of sharing plates with Chloe and Greg) and a bottle of cava. As the bubbly was being poured, Greg and Katie launched right back into talk of finance and accounting, and while I had a business degree and years of experience running them, they might as well have been speaking a different language.

Chloe made sure I didn't feel like an awkward third wheel. "I didn't know you *owned* that bar," she said once she learned about my plans to open the speakeasy. "That changes my opinion of you."

"For the better, I hope?"

"Oh, definitely." She leaned in, her whisper husky. "You see, I have a rule. I don't put out on a first date with bartenders."

Her pale blue eyes were like a wildcat's, homing in on its prey. I managed not to gulp. "And business owners?"

"Well, maybe you'll find out," she winked.

I chanced a look at Katie, wondering how she'd take the flirtation. If she'd heard, she didn't show it. She had her chin resting on her elbow as she listened. Guilty lust squeezed around my chest as I ran with Chloe's suggestion. The four of us were clicking. I could see this going further.

But I said the smarter thing. "I seriously doubt it. We agreed..." I glanced at Katie, letting Chloe know which *we* I was talking about. "This was just dinner. Just a conversation."

"Of course, of course." Chloe scooped up her wine and took a sip. "But Greg and I were talking on our way over here. We have a proposal that I think you'll like."

"I don't know—"

"It's not what you think. Trust me." The blonde pushed back from the table. "Excuse me, I have to use the lady's room."

Katie rose with her as though asked directly to join. To Greg, she said, "We'll continue this later, but I *do* think ethics plays an important part in corporate finance."

"You'll have to have a pretty convincing argument," he said, leaning back in his chair. We watched them go before Greg turned to me. "Your wife is incredible."

"Thanks. Believe me, I know."

Greg went on, like he had to prove it. "She's not only beautiful, but she's incredibly smart. And successful. Successful women hold a special place in my heart."

"Like Chloe?"

"It's one of the first things that attracted me to her." Greg re-filled our glasses—wine this time, the cava was long gone. "You and Chloe seem to be getting along."

We were, although unlike Greg and Katie, we weren't bonding over mutual interests beyond what our spouses were doing. Remembering Greg's kink, though, I decided to feed it a little. "Chloe's great. You're a lucky man, my friend"

"You can be, too, you know. Any time. I know she's up for it." He swirled his drink. "So she told me you and Katie were curious about our lifestyle?"

Here it was: the talk. The real reason we were here. We'd been nibbling at these small plates long enough that I almost convinced myself that I was satisfied.

"Yeah, I guess so," I said.

"And you two have never done something like this before?"

"Never. I actually never even considered it until you and Chloe walked into my bar."

Greg smiled. "And now it's all you can think about. Like an obsession."

I nodded. This man knew exactly how I felt. It was weird, after living with the fantasy in my head for so long, to find a kindred spirit. "I know that it's wrong, but—"

"It's not wrong. It's not part of the social norm, but that doesn't make it *wrong*." Greg paused, organizing his thoughts. He'd already had years to work out the twisted logic of this set-up. "You and Katie love each other. I'm a good judge of people, but anyone can see that."

"I do. Which is why this is so crazy. I mean, I'm not worried about her leaving me."

"Right. You shouldn't. I don't with Chloe."

I went on, encouraged. "But then I think about her going out dancing—about meeting someone else. She gets caught up in the moment. Does something she regrets—"

"And comes home to you and tells you all about it. That's what this kink is about."

"But what if she doesn't?" It was a question I didn't even know I'd been worrying about until I blurted it out like that. Hearing it aloud, it crystallized a lot of my fears.

Greg grinned. "For me, those are the hottest encounters."

"How do you mean?"

"It's those encounters that I *think* Chloe's having that actually turn me on the most," he said, leaning back as if that explained it all.

I shook my head. "Still not following."

"I've watched Chloe fuck about ten separate guys since we've started. Sometimes, I just watch her get picked up in a bar and hear about it later—like what you saw."

"I remember."

"Bet you think about it all the time." Greg nodded. "Some-times, we've been together when she fucked them. I'd like to say that those are the hottest, except that they're not."

I suddenly knew where this was going, and with the cold sense of horror, I realized that I understood it.

Greg continued. "The hottest encounters are the ones I don't know about. The ones she's had without telling me. The ones I can only ever speculate on. I travel a lot for work, and I know that Chloe doesn't spend all her time alone. It's the *possibility* that really turns me on. Not the actual act. She could be home knitting for all I care—although I'm pretty sure that's not what's going on. But you know what? As fucked up as some people would think it is, we love each other. And that makes it all okay."

So many of the things he was saying resonated with me, yet I still couldn't accept it all. "But she's sleeping around on you…"

"Maybe?" Greg waved his hand in front of him. "But that's not really the point. The point is that she's not doing it because there's something wrong with our relationship. Love and sex are two very different things. At the end of the day, Chloe loves me, and only me. Everything else is just fun."

I just nodded, unsure of what else to say.

Greg nodded back, then pushed on. "Hey, after this, Chloe and I were wondering if you'd be up for this little night club downtown for some dancing?"

"Oh, I don't dance." And this was starting to creep into terri-tory that was tempting, but well out of what Katie and I had talked about.

"I don't either," Greg said, shaking his head. "I was thinking we'd actually hang back here for a drink, let the girls make their arrival without us, and then we'd follow to watch."

Now that was a plan that got my blood pumping.

"Don't over think it. That's what I did, and I lost a lot of time." He glanced past me. Katie and Chloe must be on their way back. "Tonight, just go with the flow."

I turned in my seat, following Greg's eyes. Chloe stood slightly in front of Katie, her red-painted lips curled up in a smile. "So you boys up for a little game?"

****

Greg and I sipped our way through two fingers of expensive tequila, despite the almost irresistible urge to throw it back and drink it all in one go. I'd been working in bars patronized by college kids too long. My appreciation for fine liquor had been thoroughly desensitized.

Also, somewhere out there, Katie was getting hit on by strangers.

"The first time it happened was totally unplanned, as they always are." With just us guys left, we'd moved to the bar and Greg was suddenly moved to tell me his life story. I forced myself to listen, even as my thoughts strayed to Katie...straying.

"It was at a bachelorette party." Greg chuckled to himself. "I know, how cliché, right? Her younger sister, Kelly, was getting married and wanted her last hurrah to be over-the-top. Kelly's calmed down in the last few years, but she's always been pretty wild—and her friends were way worse."

I interrupted—habit of a bartender to appear engaged. "So they fit right in with Chloe."

Greg barked a laugh. "Not at all. Believe it or not, but Chloe's always been the responsible one. I think part of that came from watching the shit-show her little sis put on. Chloe's driven. She knows what she wants and goes for it, that's all. Back then, we'd tossed around my fantasy a little, but it was all in the guise of being *just a fantasy.*" He put air quotes around the last.

"I think that's where Katie and I are now." The bartender instincts in me fell away. Now it was just me, Max, interested in this conversation.

"It's a fucking confusing place to be. Trust me, it's not one I miss." He swirled his drink. "Anyway, so she was organizing this bachelorette party for her sister—and hating that she had to do it the whole time. I offered up our place since I'd been scheduled to be out of town. The plan was that they go out, get trashed somewhere, and finish the party in the safety of our place.

"Everything's set, the day comes, and my trip gets cancelled. No big deal, right? Our house is large enough that I can just hide away in the back rooms and stay out of the way. Well, when they come back, close to 2, they're all shit-faced—including Chloe. Not only that, but they have all these guys in tow."

I knew where this was going. I felt my gut tighten for Greg. "Okay," I said.

"I just hid in the back, but I couldn't not take a peek. Dude, it was the hottest thing I'd ever seen. They were gathered around the coffee table, everyone laughing and talking at once, so I couldn't understand a damn thing, you know? They'd opened a few bottles of champagne—nothing says bachelorette party than the bubbly, right? Everyone was paired up, including Chloe. She was sitting on some young stud's lap, completely at ease with his arms around her."

"You'd never talked about this before?" I said. My heart thundered.

"Not really. I mean, she knew about my fantasy, but it was always just a *fantasy*. Until it wasn't. That night proved that we could survive the transition."

"Was this one of the times she didn't tell you about?"

"Oh, no, we talked about it. A lot. She actually saw me spying on her that night. I don't think anything would have happened if she hadn't, but I can't be sure. As things started to get sloppy in the living room—like, orgy sloppy—Chloe texted me and told me to hide in our closet. We have this huge walk-in thing that gave me a direct line of sight to the bed." Greg paused, shook his head at the memory. "Good thing they're big enough to lay down in. I slept in that closet that night..."

"Wow." I had no more words.

"Yeah, right? It was so fucking intense, watching this woman you know so well—or thought you know—just give it up like that and let go. Chloe's not a timid lover, either. She told me after that the guy kept calling her for another go."

"And did they?"

Greg grinned. "Chloe said that she turned him down. I know for a fact that they fucked the next week when I was out of town."

"How?"

"Longer story, but I know people. If I'm interested in something, not much gets past me." He looked at his watch. "We better get going before the girls give up and let some guys entice them home."

I liked to think I knew the majority of clubs around, but the basement bar we ducked into was completely off my radar. I'd expected a total dive joint, so was very surprised by the smoked glass lounge we entered. It was dark yet friendly, with a cozy little dance floor to match. It was also packed to the corners and hot despite the winter night outside.

"This wasn't what I was expecting," I said.

Greg nodded over to the bar. "There they are. Looks like we're just in time."

Katie and Chloe stood at the far end of the bar, flanked by a couple attractive guys. Both guys were Latin, tall and square-jawed like they'd just walked off the set of a telenovela. A part of me laughed at how generic this was; the rest of me was a quivering mess.

Over the years, I'd learned a few things about Katie's preferences. She so rarely shared them with anyone that I savored each like an expensive chocolate. First, she'd confessed that she liked European guys—something about their accent, dark hair and dark skin.

Judging from how he towered over Katie, even in her heels, he had at least a few inches on me, with wide shoulders and a thicker upper body. Once, when we were both drunk and watching some softcore show on Cinemax, she'd let on that she liked the broad and the muscled. In the light of the day, she'd always maintained that she liked svelte guys, like me, and the few times I'd brought her confession up, she laughed it off as untrue.

For Katie, though, none of it mattered if there wasn't confidence. Not when we were talking about purely physical attraction. As I watched this guy pull her out onto the dance floor, his hand splayed across her lower back, I knew this guy had it, and had it in spades.

"Now that dude is a lucky SOB," Greg said. He was looking at Katie, not his own wife. Oddly, it was Greg's look that set off the butterflies more than anything. I pushed those thoughts into the back of my mind and focused on Katie and her new friend.

Okay, so once the butterflies had been released, watching the two spin and sway to the sultry Latin beat didn't do a thing to settle them. Katie had hips and knew exactly what to do with them on the floor, swiveling and reversing them, letting her sensual moves be led by her partner's guiding hands. Her black wrap dress rode higher up her taut thighs with each turn and spin. I caught a flash of dark stocking top before she pulled it back into place.

Greg was like the devil, whispering in my year. "Katie's up for it, you know. She's ripe."

I didn't acknowledge that I'd heard. I couldn't stop watching the two as the music changed to a slower samba. They transitioned like ballroom dancers, their feet sliding along the floor to the sinuous tune.

"I bet you she's thinking about fucking that guy right now," he continued. "I bet that all it'd take was a nod from you and she'd let herself get swept away...once she remembers you're here, I mean."

The guy dancing with her was good. He drew her close, locking eyes with my wife until nothing existed in her world but him as they moved to the slow, Latin beat.

Greg kept going, as relentless as the guy with Katie. "She told Chloe about the kiss in New York."

The memory of her confession—the kiss—still scrambled my insides. "She did?"

"I don't think either of you realize how close she really got to crossing the line back then."

"What do you mean?" Was there more to the story than what Katie had confessed? My heart seized at the possibility.

"I mean, two drunk adults, attracted to one another, alone in a strange city..."

"But they just kissed, right? Did she tell Chloe something different?"

"No, that's what she told Chloe, too. But come on, just think about it. They're both adults. She's away from home and under a lot of stress. Do you really think she just came to her senses all at once?"

Greg was right. Anything could have happened. In fact, it seemed more plausible that more had occurred than hadn't. "I need to ask her."

"Want my advice?" he asked. I didn't think that I did, but listened anyway. "Don't. Let it lie. Isn't it hotter not knowing, anyway?"

I didn't want to answer that question, not to Greg. Not even to myself. "I'll think about it."

"Don't worry. I have a feeling she's going to have something new to confess soon. Tonight even, if you'd just let it happen."

The guy whispered something into Katie's ear—something that brought a smile to her face. She shook her head, but that didn't seem to put the guy off. He spun her to face away, then pulled her ass against his pelvis. Brushing her hair away to bare her neck, he tried again.

Katie smiled, looked out across the bar, and found me in the crowd.

Was this my cue? Was she expecting me to nod? To somehow say, *I'm okay if you want to fuck him*, all in a look? Even if I could, I wasn't sure I wanted that.

Making sure the guy's attention was on Katie—which it was—I mouthed, *I love you*. Was I giving permission? Would she take it that way?

When she replied with a silent, *I love you, too,* panic set it as I worried that she had. She turned to the guy and set her hand on his broad chest. With her back to me, all I could see was the man's face. If he was in the process of being rejected, he sure didn't act like it. He smiled a toothy, too-handsome smile, skimmed a hand down her arm until their fingers entwined, and nodded.

He spun her one last time before they parted. He went his way—back to the bar—she came ours.

"What?" Greg asked when he saw my smile.

You can't plan for epiphanies. Inspiration isn't something that can be switched on and poured like a tap. For months, I'd been waiting for it to arrive with the name of my speakeasy. Six months out from opening and my PR people were getting nervous that it still didn't have one. Now, it had arrived.

"I think I know what I'm going to call my new bar," I said. I watched as Katie picked her way through the crowd, drawing stares like a boat leaves a wake. She was the woman that others secretly wanted to be. She was the girl-next-door with a naughty secret.

"You going to share, man?" Greg said.

"Not yet." My eyes never left my wife.

In my head, I was already imagining the placard with the bar's name on it, understated brass like the one I saw in New York. The more I thought about the name, the more I knew it was perfect. I'd call it: *The Katherine*.

"We ready to call it a night?" Greg asked as Katie stepped up to us.

"I'm ready to go home, but not to call it a night," Katie said suggestively.

Greg laughed. "Our ride should be outside. Why don't you two head out first. I'll get Chloe."

I didn't know what he was talking about with *our ride*, but Katie seemed to, moving through the crowd with purpose. I followed until we were back out in the freezing air. Sitting at the curb was a sleek black stretch limo.

I turned to Katie. "Our ride?"

Katie nodded. "Chloe and I took it over here earlier. They're intent on showing us a good time."

A man in a black suit hopped out and opened the door for us. Even inside, the chill of the night lingered. We huddled against one another at the front end of the limo as we waited for Greg and Chloe to join us. Outside, the world went on past the tinted windows. It wasn't quite midnight; the going-out crowd was just hitting its stride.

"So are we?" I asked. "Having a good time, I mean?"

Katie shivered, whether from memory or cold, I wasn't sure. "Yeah. Did you?"

"Yeah." I kissed her forehead. "It was very sexy. *You* were very sexy."

"You're not upset?" she asked.

I guided her hand down the front of my pants. She felt my erection and nodded.

"No, I'm not upset." I'd had enough to drink that the next question was easy to ask. "Did you want to fuck him?"

She squeezed my cock before releasing it. "You wish I did."

"I do, but that's not the question. Do you?"

Katie kissed me before answering. "It was all I could think about. From the moment I met him in the bar."

The door opened and in ducked Chloe. "Well, well. Hope we're interrupting something, kiddos."

Katie yanked her hand away. Even in the dark, the gesture wasn't lost on the blonde.

"Don't stop on my account," she said. Greg ducked in behind her, his hand on her lower back.

"Don't stop what?" he asked.

"Seems our new friends can't wait to get home." Chloe and Greg settled into the bend toward the back of the limo, opposite us. Greg draped his arm around Chloe, who snuggled up against him, her shapely legs crossed.

"I feel the same way," Greg said. He kissed Chloe's cheek, but his eyes angled toward us. "When I found this one, she had her tongue shoved down some guy's throat as his hands groped her ass."

Chloe looked up at him, a glint in her eye. "Don't worry, Greg. I got his number. I told him I couldn't wait to feel him inside me…"

Greg grinned. To us, he said, "See what she does to me?"

Chloe squirmed back against him. "God, I'm so horny, and you're fucking hard."

"You always make me hard, baby."

They were so natural with each other that I almost couldn't believe they weren't practically humping just a few feet from us. The limo had pulled away at some point. The city lights slid by.

"Katie looked like she was doing pretty well, too," Greg commented.

Chloe nuzzled back against him, her breasts spilling dangerously over the top of the strapless dress. "I saw that. I've been out with her twice now, and I'm beginning to notice a trend in the kinds of guys she likes."

"That's just coincidence." Katie hadn't pulled her hand away from me, but she was still pressed close.

"What was?" Chloe said. "That they were both Latin? Or that they were built?"

"The Latin thing," she admitted.

I found my voice first. "So you like the muscles thing, huh? I'm going to have to start hitting the gym more."

"Don't be silly. I love you the way you are," Katie said.

Chloe added, "But variety is *always* nice."

"Sorry the night didn't end the way you were hoping," Greg said. The apology sounded strange after hanging out with the alpha all night long.

Chloe's eyes caught in the light of a passing street lamp. She was staring right at me. "It's not too late."

My chest tightened. My cock strained. I wished I hadn't had so much to drink. I wished that I could think straight. For an instant, all I could think about was Chloe crawling across the limo floor and settling her head between my legs.

Katie rescued me, only a touch of jealousy mixed in her voice. "You're not coming onto my man, are you?"

Chloe smiled, her eyes flicking over to my wife. "Of course not. There are a lot of things we can do without actually sharing…"

As if choreographed, Greg reached up and pushed the strapless top of Chloe's dress down, baring her chest. It was dark, but this I couldn't miss. Her coral-hued nipples sat hard and high on her small tits. No bra. She didn't need one.

I couldn't formulate any words. All I could do was watch as I tried to figure out how I should feel. Should I be excited by it? Should I be worried about what Katie thought of it?

Chloe shifted to the side, her hand worked down between Greg's legs as his mouth closed over a nipple. When Chloe fished Greg's cock out of his fly, semi-erect and already huge, I heard Katie's breath catch. I glanced at her as she squirmed a little, squeezing her thighs in that universal *I'm aroused* way.

My attention darted back to Chloe and Greg as I watched Chloe shift back up into Greg's lap. She reached beneath her short dress, and a moment later her thong decorated the floor of the limo. She aligned her hips with his, then gasped through her wide smile. Was this really happening? Were they fucking right in front of us?

"Sorry to be rude, but I couldn't wait," Chloe said. She braced herself on Greg's knees as his hands covered her tits. "And besides, I really like to be watched."

I didn't know what to do. I squeezed Katie closer to me, taking comfort in knowing that I wasn't by myself. She seemed to remember that I was there, turning to look at me with the same wild look in her eyes that I felt. *Is this really happening?!*

"You know, I like to watch, too," Chloe said. When I looked over at her, I realized she was saying it *to me*. I knew what I had to do.

I pulled Katie in for a hard kiss. She welcomed it, devouring my tongue as she shoved hers down my throat. We turned into each other, knees touching. I slid my hand up the inside of her thigh and found the silky lace I'd glimpsed earlier. She kept her knees locked together. At first. All it took was a few kisses along her neck and the back of her ear and I had enough access to crawl up the bare skin of her upper thigh.

She was dripping by the time I pushed my fingers inside her thong. I easily curled two fingers between her slippery folds. She clutched at my thigh and the edge of her seat as a quiet moan slipped free. By the time I was done, I wanted her screaming.

Chloe beat her to the punch. "FUCK ME!" the blonde cried out.

Keeping my fingers sliding in and out of Katie and my head laid against her shoulder, I looked across at the other couple. Chloe had pushed her dress up over her hips. Nothing hid Greg's monster as he slid it in and out of Chloe's bald snatch.

She reached back and pulled Greg close for a sloppy, open-mouthed kiss. He squeezed her tits from behind, twisting her nipples hard enough that she had to break the kiss with a moaned, "*FUCK!*" Then she really started to fuck Greg.

I'd never seen such carnality only a few feet from me. Her tight little body glistened as street lamps strobed across it. We were on the highway. I vaguely noticed. Other cars slid by us in the night. Did they have any idea what was going on inside the limo just beside them? Could they have guessed that they'd see this if the windows came down?

Chloe panted with each cock-length bounce. "Fuck... me... fuck... ME... FUCKME FUCKMEEE!"

Katie's fingers on my zipper drew my attention back to her.

"I need you," she whispered. My belt clasp clacked through the confined space. Together, we yanked my pants and boxers down as I crawled over her. She pulled her thong to the side as I placed my cockhead against her. "I *need* you," she repeated.

I sank to my balls in one fluid motion.

"You two are so hot!" Chloe mewed. She and Greg had slowed their vigorous screw session to watch us perform. The snug grip on my cock quivered as Katie was reminded of our audience.

My cock swelled. I pumped harder. With one knee on the bench of the limo and my hands grasping the back of it, I leveraged all my weight into each thrust.

Katie screamed. The walls of her pussy pulsed around my cock, a siren's call to come crashing along these shores. With one final thrust, I did, erupting inside Katie's welcoming body in the presence of another couple.

"Fucking A, that was hot," Chloe said behind me. "Now I'm definitely envious of you, Katie."

I pulled free, first checking on Katie to make sure that she was okay. Her face was bright red and her eyes were wide, but she didn't seem like she was about to go into hysterics. She deftly smoothed her skirt down as I zipped back up, like there was a point to preserving our modesty anymore.

Mercifully, Chloe and Greg had finished and were once again covered. Chloe sat snuggled against her husband, her legs folded up beneath her. If I ignored the smell of sex and Chloe's lacy thong on the floor, it was almost like nothing had happened.

Only everything had happened.

Katie spoke when I could not. "I don't think I can handle my alcohol like I used to. Did that just happen?"

When she laughed, we all did. The tension burned away. I could breathe again.

Chloe touched Greg's leg lovingly and looked at him. "We've done that a few times before, but it's never been that intense, has it, honey?"

Greg nodded. "Never."

Chloe went on. "I hope we didn't freak you out. Sometimes I forget that not everyone's as...erm, open-minded as us."

"No, no," Katie and I said in unison, neither of us quite telling the truth.

"Good, because we like you two. Tonight was so much fun, even before the kinky stuff."

Greg added, "We haven't clicked like this with another couple in a while. I hope we can do it again some time."

The way he looked at Katie sent my stomach doing flips.

"Me, too." Katie and I spoke over each other again, this time with more sincerity.

"Katie, I'll call you Monday," Chloe said. "We still need to finalize a few things about the building sale."

"Have a good night, you two," Greg added.

It was only then that I realized that the limo wasn't moving— that it had stopped on our sleepy suburban street. That our *normal* life was just up the lamp-lined walk. Greg and Chloe didn't get out, but we all hugged awkwardly in the low space, including a hushed, "I'll be in touch," from Chloe.

Katie and I stood stunned in the cold as we watched the limo drive away, like a dirty version of Cinderella's story at the end of her night with the prince.

Katie huddled close, looking up at me with a raised brow. "So just dinner?"

We burst out laughing.

"Come on," I said. "Let's get inside and pay off the babysitter."

"You know, I'm not really tired…" Katie said.

"Good. Me either."

That night, we didn't talk much about the wild experience, but we didn't sleep much, either.

CHAPTER 8

We both woke up feeling like the Macy's Day Parade had marched into our skulls. My mouth was dry. My body was still sheathed in a booze-fueled numbness. I didn't get sick, but I kind of wished that I had.

Katie got sick. Then she crashed again.

Now the difference between being hung over when you're just a couple versus a parent is that your kid doesn't really have enough sympathy to let you sleep. Mya came charging in at some ungodly hour—that turned out to be just before 9. I was pretty sure that I'd had less to drink than Katie, so I dragged myself out of bed to make our daughter oatmeal and bacon.

Things got better with coffee—doesn't everything? My body still ached and I still couldn't clear all the cobwebs, but I started to remember what we'd done last night. Not that that made any more sense. Had we really done that? Had we had sex in front of another couple as they had sex? Seemed plausible in a dream-like way until

I considered who my wife was. She abhorred strip clubs, pornography, and the idea of acting slutty. Had she really unzipped me? Had she whispered, *I need you?*

Katie came downstairs a couple hours later, looking better than she had a right to. Mya was watching *Dora the Explorer* and I was slumped over my third cup of coffee.

"Hey," she said. "I had the craziest dream..." Katie said. She ran her hand through her hair and shook her head.

"Me, too." We shared a laugh. "Did that really happen?"

Katie plopped down at the kitchen table and took a sip of my coffee. "I think so? I remember having dinner. Then dancing. Then..."

"Yeah," I said. I reached out and covered her hand, squeezing her fingers. "Then the limo."

Katie looked down at our entwined hands. Her eyes cut back up at me through her long lashes. "That was hot."

"Yeah." And Katie telling me she felt that way was even hotter. "I couldn't believe it when you unzipped me."

"I did?" She looked up and away, as if trying to remember. Her faint smile told me that she did. "God, I'm sorry."

"Why? Don't apologize. It was incredible."

"I was so horny. I couldn't stop myself. It was like I was possessed or something."

"You should get possessed more often," I said. "So we're good?"

"I wouldn't use that word, but yeah, I'm okay with it." Katie fingered my coffee mug as she organized her thoughts. "I still can't believe...well, any of it. But I don't regret it."

"Chloe and Greg are pretty wild, huh?"

She said, "Now there's an understatement."

"Do we like them?"

"Yes, I think we do. There's something dangerous about them, but—"

I finished for her. "But maybe that's what's so exciting about them." Katie nodded. "Do you think Greg's attractive?"

Her admission was only a little hesitant. "Yeah, but if this is going where I think it is..." She took a deep breath. "I don't think I'm ready to try, you know, *swinging* or anything." Her face was as bright as her hair.

"I'd be fine just watching," I said. I couldn't help it. The words tumbled out like a compulsion.

"How's that, Max? What's in it for you?" We'd been down this road countless times.

I still didn't have a clear answer, but I could try.

"It's never been about me being with another woman. What turns me on is you and another man. That's what gets me dizzy with excitement. I don't even need to be there—although that would be awesome. Even just knowing what you were up to would drive me crazy."

Katie chewed on that. Before she could come up with something to say, Mya started calling for another episode of Dora. Life as a suburbanite came storming back.

****

A week later, Katie walked into the house still on the phone, just back from the office. She laughed. "Oh, you're nuts, you know that?"

I waved at her from the kitchen, where Mya and I were putting together a puzzle on the table (for the fifth time that half hour). Katie tucked her phone between her head and shoulder and hung her coat in the closet. There was nothing particularly sexy about her black suit—the skirt brushed her knees and the pink blouse she wore beneath was standard business wear—but I found myself stirring regardless.

"Okay, okay..." she said, still talking into the phone. She reached back and released her hair from its bun. It fell in rich, auburn waves as she shook it out. She fixed a look, right at me. "I'll talk to him. Bye now."

She ended the call, laughed, and gave the two of us a big smile.

"What was that about?" I asked.

"That was Chloe. I'll talk to you about it later."

"Mommy, come help us put the princess puzzle together!" Mya said. She placed the last puzzle piece into its spot, looked up at us like she'd just solved world peace, then flipped the puzzle board over. "Mommy, come on. Help!"

"*Please*, Mya? Remember to say please." Despite the dark suit, Katie had already shifted into mom mode.

"Pleeease?!"

Katie laughed and sat down next to us. "Okay, kiddo. Let's start with the corners..."

It wasn't until Mya was asleep that I got the skinny on the phone conversation, and if I'd known what she was holding back, I wouldn't have been able to focus on a thing. We were in bed, me in just my boxers and Katie in a t-shirt and long, satin pajama pants. The smooth material slithered across my bare legs as she got close.

"Would you be mad if I went to an art show this Friday?" she said. I started to ask why I'd be mad when she added, "With Greg?"

My heart jumped. "Alone?"

Katie nodded, rushing ahead as her face flushed. "They'd planned on going to some big gallery opening on Friday a while back, but something came up and Chloe has to travel that weekend. She thought it was silly for him to go alone and they thought of me."

"I bet they *thought* of you."

"Oh, this is silly. Never mind."

"No, I'm sorry. It's not silly. It…well, it's really sexy." I kissed her gently. She tasted minty from her toothpaste, so familiar, yet still full of surprises. Here she was, intrigued by this offer to spend time alone with Greg—our best option to explore my fantasy further—and here I was trying to sabotage it.

"I think you should go," I said. "It'll be fun."

"You sure?" she asked. We both knew she wasn't asking whether I was sure about her attending the art show. She was asking if I was sure about taking this to the next level. To reiterate, she added, "You think we're ready for that?"

"I think so."

She stared up at me and I saw the uncertainty mixed with desire that I felt etched in her face. When she spoke, it was like rising out of water. "I think so, too."

****

The few days leading up to the gallery opening felt like a heat wave that would never end—despite the freeze outside. Our lovemaking was rabid every night, like we had to prove that no matter what happened on Friday, we still loved each other.

Katie came home Friday afternoon to get ready, a mix of shopping bags in tow. I'd already dropped Mya off at my parents' house so I could sweat the evening alone.

Her auburn hair looked different, burnished like copper when the light caught it. It fell in loose waves around her shoulders, giving her a Fifties starlet look. She noticed me looking.

"I had a little taken off the ends, and got it blown out." Her nails had been polished, too: French tips that I always loved.

"Someone took a detour on the way home from work."

"I took off after lunch to take care of a few things." She smelled like an Aveda spa, which suggested something else.

"A few things?" I asked.

"No, not that," she said, touching my nose. "I had my waxing appointment yesterday. Don't want to be too sensitive for tonight."

Katie's laugh was delightful.

Watching her prepare for her night out with another man turned me inside out. She applied her makeup wearing nothing but the lingerie she'd planned to wear, explaining that she didn't want to get her dress messy (although I was pretty sure she was just doing it to tease me).

Her luxuriously soft lace lingerie was predominantly black, with red scrolls and fringing to give it a classic feel. The bra was a push-up, something that she rarely wears on account of the size of her breasts. They do such a good job that her freckled cleavage looks practically store bought, something she'd always called trampy. Not tonight, apparently. She even added a multi-string diamond necklace that drew my eyes down into her mouth-watering bust.

A matching garter belt held her black, patterned stockings high on her thighs, and a thong completed the look. She ran a pencil along her dark, trimmed brows, then met my eyes in the mirror.

"Honey, could you get the shoes out of the Bloomingdale's bag?"

Uncomfortably hard, I did as I was told, retreating from the doorway where I was probably leering a little too much. I found the mess of bags at the foot of the bed and a shoebox emblazoned with Jimmy Choo's name—she really had gone all out for this evening. I let that thought steep for a moment as I picked through her other bags. Hidden inside the Bloomingdale bag was a plastic CVS bag.

Seeing it was like uncovering a hissing snake, coiled and ready to strike. I sucked in breath so fast I felt dizzy. I knew what was in there, but looked anyway. I hadn't seen a box of Trojans since before I'd met Katie; she'd always been on the pill and we never worried about any further protection. There'd been no reason to buy them... until now.

The reality of the night hit home. This was no longer some kind of game. My wife was going to have sex with someone else. After the initial shock, my pulse calmed down to comfortable levels. I didn't feel the sting of jealousy I'd been expecting. It was there, of course— I'd thought about it enough to realize that the jealousy was a healthy indicator of my feelings—but it didn't cripple my thoughts.

Katie called from the bathroom and I jumped, slipping the CVS bag back into the other.

"You find them, honey?" she said.

"Um, yeah." I pulled the Jimmy Choos out, gawking at their height. "Wow, are you going to be able to walk in them?"

Katie laughed. "Tell me about it. The woman helping me out convinced me *I had to have them*. I'll make sure to send her my medical bill when I break my ankle."

It seemed so weird, chatting with her like this. Like this was any normal day. Like she was getting ready for a date with me. I watched her line her lips with deep, ruby red. Would she be wrapping those same lips around Greg later tonight?

She stood and blew me a kiss. She looked as nervous as she was excited. "How do I look?"

"Like a pin-up model."

Katie went back to her bags, her tits spilling out of her bra as she leaned over. I could almost see her nipples at the edge of the cups of the bra. "I went little and black," she said, holding up a scrap of black cloth that looked much too small to be a dress.

In front of the mirror, she shimmied into the slinky black material, tugging it here and there until it was in place.

"Zip me up?" She gave me her back. The dress ended about mid-thigh, but a slit up the back was high enough that it could show the tops of her stockings if you looked closely enough.

"Wow, this is tight." I ran my hand along the curves that the dress accentuated more than hid. My jaw dropped when she turned around. With her push-up bra and the low plunge of the scooped front, her chest was completely on display.

"You think it's too much?" Reading her smile, she knew the answer to her question.

"It's perfect."

Katie spun, demonstrating that she could maneuver in her heels after all. She looked neither slutty nor trashy, and she was far from cheap, despite the display of décolletage. She looked like arm-candy.

"Think Greg will approve?" she teased.

"I think he's going to have a hard time keeping his hands off you."

Katie's eyes flared. "I hope so."

"You're killing me."

She stepped close. In her heels, she was practically my height. "You love it," she said.

"I do. And I love you."

She toyed with my collar. "You sure about this? Last chance to back out."

"I am. I want you to have a good time." Color touched her cheeks, which were already touched up with blush. She'd done a good job with makeup, applying it naturally, even when she applied a lot. She looked good enough to go to the Oscars. "But Katie, anything that happens tonight...I want you to tell me after, okay?"

"Then maybe nothing will happen." She kissed my nose, careful not to smear her lipstick. "Or maybe I won't see you until the morning."

I didn't know what jumped more, my cock or my heart rate.

"Now go and call me a cab," Katie said. "I think I'm ready."

"Yes, ma'am."

When she was gone, I crept back into the bedroom. My face was on fire as I returned to the CVS bag. The box of condoms was still there, but it was open and half-empty.

I released a long breath in the hope that it would calm my galloping heart. That was wishful thinking. I set the bag back where it was and backed away, my mind flying a mile a minute. What had she felt when she'd stepped up to the CVS counter with that box in her hand? Probably something similar to the way I was feeling now.

"Okay," I said aloud to the empty room. "This is happening. This is *happening*." *She's out there, on her way to meet up with another man—a man we'd watched have sex right in front of our eyes—without a curfew, and with half a dozen latex reasons not to come home.*

This is happening!

I floated into the office, my head clogged and confused, and booted up the computer. I didn't even know what I was doing until my fingers started typing.

It was an easy thing to find: directions to the gallery opening. I could have texted Chloe, but I was done with that flirtation with danger. The Internet was safer, and more anonymous.

I knew the gallery name—it was in a warehouse-turned-gallery on the east side, in this new artist's hamlet. The artist was a woman by the name of Adrienne Ormond who specialized in nude, black and white photography. Apparently, the opening was a big one—biggest to date for that neighborhood.

Sending Mya to the grandparents was probably a mistake, I thought as I maneuvered my car onto the interstate without much of a plan. Then I shoved those doubts down and made my way to the opening.

Turns out, the *biggest opening ever* was both a blessing and a curse. I almost didn't get in, having to talk my way past the door attendant. Once in, though, it was crowded enough that I could blend in and observe without fear of being spotted. The gallery space was expansive and filled to capacity. The ceilings were high and the white walls bare to accommodate the blown up prints of males and females in various states of undress. Many were abstract enough that I didn't realize what I was looking at until I stepped back. Then everything came into focus. Funny how that works.

I didn't spend my time looking at art, though. I was here with a purpose, and I spent the first ten minutes searching for it. When I didn't find them, I started to worry. Had I missed them? Was I going to run into them rounding a corner. I moved from room to room, always making a wide berth through each door. I sipped the white wine being served on the trays, ate the passed hors d'oeuvres, and nodded at people that I made eye contact with. But everyone seemed to recognize that I was on my way *somewhere.*

I found Greg and Katie in one of the largest rooms of the gallery and, thankfully, also one of the most crowded. They were standing close, hips touching, heads tilted into one another as they discussed the scandalous photo in front of them. The contrast was low and the lighting fuzzy, but it still very clearly depicted the bare and slightly engorged labia of a woman, catching the crook of her thigh and the subtle V of her hipbone. Contributing to the clean look of all the photographs, the model had no pubic hair, making this piece even more striking.

It was thrilling to watch Katie so uninhibited with another man. It made me jealous, sure, but my feelings were so much more complex than just that. Katie reached out and touched Greg's elbow to emphasize a point. When she listened, she nodded attentively, smiled up at him, touched her hair. She only touched her hair when she was nervous. Or horny.

Greg led her to the next photo, his hand brushing dangerously low on his back. Did he feel her garter belt there? Had he felt lower?

Around and around the room they went. I did my best to watch without watching. I even got close enough to hear them speaking at one point at a particularly crowded intersection.

"So you and Max are okay with this?"

"We've talked a lot about it, but are we *okay* with this? I don't know if I'll ever be able to answer that one."

Greg smiled. "You will. Chloe and I were once like that. Now…"

Katie's laugh was something in between a sigh and a titter. "We saw what you're like now last week."

"Hope we didn't offend," Greg said.

"You didn't. Shocked, absolutely. Intrigued? Maybe. But offend, no."

Had Katie just admitted that Greg's lifestyle intrigued her? To Greg?

"You could be up on these walls, you know," he said, changing subjects. "Have you ever posed?"

"Naked? Never!" Katie laughed.

He whispered something else, but they were lost to me as they filtered out of this room. I gave them a few minutes before following, realizing that I was in the foyer where the main bar had been set up. Tall cocktail tables dotted the room, all of them filled.

Again, my heart skipped a beat when I spotted them on the far side of the room. Greg had my wife backed up in an alcove, their profiles to me through the dense filter of people. No one paid more than a glance. No one but me.

He was standing close, his knee pushed up between her thighs and his hand cradling her face. She was looking at him like he as the only thing that existed. I knew the look, but had never seen it directed at another man. He leaned forward, resting one hand on her hips as he whispered into her ear. Katie swallowed a red lip into her mouth and nodded.

He kissed her then, slow and smoldering. Even across the room, I could see their mouths open and their tongue unite. As public as this was, I still had to consciously will myself not to touch my throbbing manhood.

"I'm glad someone's getting into the mood with my work," a

woman's voice said over my shoulder. I broke free of my trance, turning to find a tall, alluring woman before me. Her dark hair hung in glossy waves around her pale beauty. "I'm Adrienne. I don't think we've met."

"Um...I'm Max," I said woodenly, too slow to make up a name.

"Hi, Max. Are you enjoying the show?"

I started to feel more comfortable, so I asked, "Which one?"

"Touché." She glanced back at Katie and Greg, who were still kissing. "She's in for the night of her life."

"I'm sorry?"

"That man she's with? Let's just say he and his wife have been inspirational to this work."

"Oh?"

"Oh."

I looked around the gallery, wondering if any of the blown-up photos were of Chloe. They were too abstract to tell.

Adrienne sipped her wine, spotted someone else she knew, and moved on.

Katie and Greg were on the move, too. He was helping Katie into her coat and I suddenly realized this was it. No more following. No more watching. After this moment, my Katie was on her own. Last chance to stop it all. Last chance while I was still a player in this game.

I just stood there and watched them leave. Stiffly, I had another drink and then went home to my empty house.

****

I could barely sleep that night, although I certainly tried. This time, I didn't wait up for her on the living room couch. For some reason, I decided to pretend like this was any other night when she was away traveling. I did my routine, brushing my teeth and washing my face. I ended up laughing at how absurd the whole night had turned out.

Every time I let my eyes close, I wondered where Katie was and what she was doing. Did they go dancing after they left? Or did they just go back to his place and fuck?

A new feeling crept in. A bad feeling. Was this right? Had I made a big mistake? Was that *hope* that I felt when I considered that maybe nothing had happened?

In bed, I tossed and turned. The hours ticked by, slowly crushing that feeble hope that tonight would remain innocent. My cock was never soft, even after I'd relieved the tension. All it took was the thought of what Katie and Greg and I was erect again.

At last, I heard the familiar sound of keys in the front door. My wife had returned. I checked the alarm clock. It was almost 5.

I lay in bed quietly as she came in. I half expected her to shower, but when she started stripping out of her dress, tossing the expensive thing on the floor, I wondered whether anything had happened at all.

My cock jerked when I realized she didn't have any lingerie to take off under the dress. No bra, no panties. Not even her stockings and garter belt. All she had to remove, after dropping the dress on the floor, were her shoes and her jewelry.

Naked, she curled under the sheets with me and kissed me on the cheek. Her hair was wet and she smelled like fresh soap. She'd already showered.

Which meant she had something to wash away.

Which meant I was growing hard again, despite having cum twice already.

"You're home," I said sleepily, pretending to have just woken up.

"Shh, honey, go back to sleep."

"Did you...?"

"In the morning, Max." She sounded very tired, I realized. "I'll tell you all about it in the morning."

****

I woke Saturday morning to an empty bed, feeling the same way I did when Katie was traveling and I was disconnected from her. Only I knew she was here. Downstairs. Waiting to talk to me. Waiting to confess.

I heard her on the phone before I got to the bottom of the stairs. I was about to step into the opening when she said, "Chloe, you're nuts!"

Something about her scandalized tone made me pause and my ears prick up. I held my breath and listened.

"Yes, we had a *very* good time..."

More than just my ears pricked up.

"Yes, you have a very nice home. And I particularly love the shower. God, do you guys really need all those shower heads?" Katie laughed again. "You're right, getting clean *is* important."

I remembered Katie's freshly washed scent when she came in last night. It occurred to me that she probably had Greg in there helping her.

"Yes, in the master bedroom… Now I see the appeal for having a giant mirror on one side of the room." She broke out laughing.

"Okay, if you're sure you're okay hearing it… Watching myself cross the line like that made it all so surreal. I mean, the first time, I was just caught up in the moment, right? We were all over each other as soon as the door was shut. Things happened so fast that. One second we were kissing. The next he had his cock buried inside of me..."

Jesus!

"But the second time, we took it slower. I was on top, facing the mirror, and watched it all happen. It was...amazing."

I stepped out into the open, unable to stay hidden any more. Katie didn't jump. Didn't look ashamed. She swung her green eyes up to mine, her smile reflected in them.

"Oh yeah, I came," she said. "I don't know how many times. It was so different, you know? So exciting." She held her hand out to me. I went over to her, taking it as she continued her conversation. "We took a couple breaks, but most of the time, we were having sex."

I was close enough that I caught snippets of what Chloe was saying. I heard something about being a slut. Katie just laughed.

"Look, I better go. Max just woke up."

Ask him about Friday, I thought I heard Chloe say.

"I will. I'll talk to you later. Bye now."

Bye.

She hung up.

"Friday?" I asked.

"She wants to meet for drinks. You, me, and Greg."

I raised my eyebrows. "Just drinks?"

The blushing woman, uncertain of even having dinner with Chloe and Mark just a couple weeks ago, was gone. "Drinks to start..."

I licked my lips. "Really?"

She snuggled into me. Her red hair had fallen over her face. She brushed it away as she looked up and said, "Really."

"Why the change?"

Katie's hand slid into mine and she pulled me back to the stairs. "Come on. Let's get more comfortable."

We went upstairs, back to the bedroom where cool morning light slanted through our wide windows. I arranged myself at the head of the bed, reclined on our pillows, as Katie stood at the foot and toyed with the buttons of her satin pajamas.

"I'm not sure how much you heard, but Greg and Chloe have this huge mirror at the foot of their bed..." She popped the buttons one by one, teasing me with the inside curve of her full breasts. "At first, I couldn't look at it. At us. It made me feel—"

"Guilty?" I prompted.

"Yeah, something like that. But not the way you might think." With the pajama shirt still on and open, she pushed her matching pants off. "My parents were pretty conservative. You know the story. I was raised to be a good girl—daddy's perfect daughter."

I did know this story. She wasn't a virgin when we met or anything (not the second time, anyway), but she'd never been a party girl, either. She'd been sweet, ready to settle down, ready to start her version of what her parents had given her.

Katie shed the pajama top and crawled onto the bed, her breasts swinging beneath her. "I kept thinking that I shouldn't be acting like I was. What would my parents say?"

"You need to put that burden down," I said. I'd been saying it for years. "Who cares what they'll never know?"

Katie stopped between my thighs. She grasped my boxers and pulled them down, unveiling the evidence of my excitement. "Don't worry, honey. By the end of the night, I was *way* past that fear."

Grasping my cock, she slid her lips over it, taking it all the way to the root without so much as a gage. She'd deep-throated me before, but she always needed some warming up. This morning, she did it with ease.

When she pulled off, her voice was hoarse. "Watching myself in the mirror like that was intense. I could pretend that it was someone else doing all those things. Someone else being naughty with this stranger."

She sucked me a few more times. I sank deep into the pillows, picturing her doing this to him.

"But you know what it really made me want?" she asked, kissing up my body.

"What?" My voice emerged just as hoarse as hers.

"I wished you had been there, watching us. God, that would have made it so sexy."

Katie rose up over me, positioned my cock against her pussy, and sank down.

"You're so wet," I groaned.

She went on, like she hadn't heard a word. "I kept thinking about how turned on you'd be if you could see what I saw. And that turned me on even more." She looked down at me. "It turns you on, doesn't it?"

"God, baby. So much." I gripped her hips as she undulated over me, watching my cock dip in and out of her slippery sex. Another man had been here just hours ago. My balls tightened. I felt like a rubber band on the threshold of snapping.

"Under that crisp business man attire, Greg's *really* fit. It was a pleasant surprise. The first time we did it, it was fast and frantic.

He was on top, smothering me with his big fucking muscles." She squirmed, lowering herself to press her tits against my chest. "The second time was slower. I got to savor it, riding him on top. *Reverse cowboy*, I think you've called it."

Hearing Katie—my sweet, somewhat conservative wife—talk to me was almost too much.

"The third time was in the shower." Pressed low on me, her voice was a whisper in my ear. "He wanted to fuck my tits, so I soaped up and did him, just the way we used to."

At some point, I crashed past the point of no return. Planting my feet on the mattress, I pressed up into her as I rode out the last moments before release.

"The last time he came—the *fourth* time—we were back in his room. He was on top with my head hanging off the side of the bed. I could see him over me. See him dominate me…"

I saw her in my feverish imagination, legs splayed and sweat-dampened hair a waterfall along the floor. I saw her cry out, a continuous orgasm getting pounded out of her by her lover's swarthy, hulking body.

She whispered against my ear, so close it felt like she was inside my head. "I wanted you to be there to watch me scream."

I erupted inside her, my fingers clamping down on the heated flesh of her buttocks. Her clipped moan grinded harsh against my ear. I felt her pussy ripple around me, milking me as her orgasm mixed with mine.

She rolled off me, sweaty and huffing as morning light bathed our naked bodies. I'd discovered a newfound love of morning sex since our adventures began. There was nothing quite like lying there with the sun warming our naked, panting bodies.

"What?" Katie asked, seeing me smiling.

"I love you, Kates. You're still amazing. You constantly surprise me."

"I constantly surprise myself," she chuckled, snuggling close. "So you're really okay with this?"

"Yeah, I really am." I said it with more confidence than I'd ever felt before. "It's crazy and insane—and I admit that it still makes me nervous when I think too hard about it—but at the end of the day, I know you're not going to leave me."

"Never," she whispered. "And if you ever get that fear, you've got to let me know."

"Of course." I could hear a bird chirping outside. How Disney of it. "So four times, huh?"

Katie shifted on me, tickling her fingers through my chest hair. "Yeah. It was impressive."

"Your first one-night stand," I said.

"Who says it's going to be a one-time thing?" Then Katie surprised me even more. "Who says it was my first?"

"What?" As far as I knew, she'd been a serial monogamous. There had been boyfriends before me—we didn't talk much about them, but I knew who they were—but never random hook-ups. "When?"

"Back in college," she began. This close, I could see Katie's skin was flushed—whether from the sex or the confession, I didn't know. "It was before you...but just before. I'd broken up with Brendan, like, two months too late. Things were bad between us, as you know. I was feeling reckless. I went with some friends to a frat party—"

"*You* went to a frat party?" I asked.

"I know, right? I even wore a tiny little dress you would have been shocked to see me in."

"Maybe not so shocked anymore," I said.

"I don't even remember his name," she went on. "I remember it was hot, I was definitely drunk. But in the morning, all I could think was: what would my parents think?"

"Do you feel that way now?"

Katie turned into me. "You know what? I don't. All I was worried about was you, Max. And even then, I wasn't so worried."

"Good, because you shouldn't be. I'm not your parents. As long as you come home to me—as long as you never stop loving me—you never have to worry about me."

"I still don't understand what you're getting out of it, Max. What's in it for you?"

And I still didn't have an answer, but since we were being honest, I'd try to come up with one. "When I saw Chloe and Greg play their game that first time, I didn't understand it either. But it was still sexy, you know? He watched her with these other guys, seeing the effect she had on them. They all wanted her, building up liquid courage, waiting for the perfect moment to pounce."

"So you wanted me to be more like Chloe?"

Danger, danger. Don't go down that road.

"Not exactly." *But yes?* "I liked her confidence, though. And I thought that if she had it, so should you."

That sounded safe. Katie chewed on it for a moment before nodding. The conversation wasn't over, just *to be continued.*

We kissed for the longest time before finally deciding it was time to be adults and face the day. Mya was at my parents' house, ready to be picked up, and I had a few things to do in preparation for The Katherine's opening.

I slipped out of bed and padded to my wardrobe, naked. When I turned back, Katie was snuggled onto her side, looking up at me through her lashes.

"What?" I asked.

Her green eyes flickered over me. "You're hot, Max."

My cock reacted. She went on.

"As long as you keep looking the way you do, you should have the same confidence as Chloe, too. And you don't ever have to worry about guys like Greg." It sounded like she was reminding herself of the fact as much as me—like she was seeing me for the first time. I knew the feeling well.

"So it's all about my looks, is it?"

"You've also got a pretty nice cock."

I returned to the bed, my erection prominent. "I think you need a reminder of my other charms."

We took our time this time, making love without talk of Greg or the fantasy. We were together, Katie and Max, and reveled in our love.

CHAPTER **9**

Despite the Art Gallery Adventure, as we'd started referring to it as, we didn't get together as a foursome immediately following. Life had to do with some of it—Katie's travel picked up again and The Katherine's opening started to swallow all my free time. Mostly, though, I think neither of us was ready to take it to that next level just yet, despite the excitement.

We relived Katie's wild night, though. Many times over the next couple months. We even purchased a mirror for the bedroom, although it wasn't as ostentatious as the one that Chloe and Max had, apparently. Still, it was fun to watch us go at it in the reflection, and if I angled it just right, with my head cut off and Katie's body rippling under me, I could imagine that it wasn't me drilling into her but someone else.

That wasn't to say that we didn't have any connection with Greg and Chloe. Katie and Chloe typically got together for lunch once a week, if she was in town. I made sure to keep my evenings open after those nights because Katie usually came in on fire.

Chloe was in touch with me, too. Every time I saw that it was her number, my heart starting beating and my conscience warned not to answer it. But I couldn't stop myself. To get a different perspective on the evolution of my wife was just too tempting.

"Katie keeps mentioning a guy named John," Chloe said during one of our conversations. "Do you know him?"

"Yeah, He's one of my manager's husband, actually. Katie and John used to work together."

"Hm...interesting."

Jealousy shifted inside of me. I thought about seeing them in New York, at The James, and Katie's reaction when I suggested she liked him. "They're just friends."

"Probably," Chloe said. *Probably.*

"Why? Did she say something?" My paranoia kicked in.

"Not really."

I tried to keep the worry out of my voice. "What is it, Chloe?"

"It's nothing. Just, well...it's nothing."

She was killing me. "Tell me. Spill it."

"I think she likes him is all. She hasn't, you know, admitted anything, but...I just have this feeling. He lives in New York?"

"Yeah. He and Nadia, his wife, have a long distance thing right now."

"Huh..." Chloe said. I didn't like the sound of that. "Probably nothing."

Probably.

I was working with Nadia more and more as we started getting serious about The Katherine's opening. The devil's in the details, they say, and Nadia was great about covering all those pesky details.

She worked with the PR firm to get our promotions ramped up. She started interviewing key staff members. We spent hours pouring over what the linens would look like, what kind of food to serve, and even what kind of music to play. It was inevitable that the conversation would swing to John and Katie eventually.

"So how are things with John?"

"As good as they can be when you only see each other on the weekends."

"Tell me about it. Sometimes, it feels like that's the only time I get to see Katie."

"Things'll settle down eventually. This is the dust settling," Nadia reassured.

"You ever worry about all the traveling? And you and him being apart?"

Nadia laughed. "Like cheating? Never crossed my mind."

I nodded. Nadia knew me well enough to know something was up.

"Don't tell me you're worried about Katie."

"I'm not." I wasn't. Why would I be? She had permission to fool around if she wanted to.

"Good. You guys are the most solid couple I know. You're an inspiration."

"Thanks."

An inspiration. Solid. That's what we were, and Katie confirmed it a week later when she told me that Greg had asked her to meet her for lunch.

"I told him no," she explained that evening. "I just don't feel comfortable doing that, you know?"

"You two seemed to hit it off," I said, drawing a sharp look from my wife. "I mean personality wise, not...physically."

Her lips curled up. "Not *just* physically."

"Right," I said, feeling my heart ignite.

"I still don't know. He wouldn't want it to be just lunch..." She bit her lip.

"Would you?"

"That's the part I really don't know. I'm awful, aren't I?" she said.

"No, you're sexy, Katie. And I'd be fine with it, too, if you wanted it to be more. Just remember to come home to me and tell me all about it."

Katie laughed nervously. "Okay, but don't hold your breath. That feels too much like a lifestyle, and that's not what I want. Besides, like I said, the next time we play, I want you there."

****

Time passed. Tax Day came and went. Katie's trips picked back up. She was gone more than she was home. We hired a nanny, finally, a wonderful older woman named Eleanor.

We celebrated our ninth anniversary early because she was going to be in London on the actual day, although we briefly considered celebrating it out there. In the end, it would be too expensive to pull off and too busy for the both of us. Katie teased me on the actual anniversary, though, texting me that she about going out dancing to *celebrate for the both of us.* The thought of her alone in a strange city drove me up the wall.

That was the thing. As time stretched out from the Art Gallery Adventure, Katie got more comfortable with the teasing. She even went dancing a couple times with Chloe, both times coming home with tales of making out with strangers on the dance floor. Chloe confirmed the stories the next day in calls that I knew I shouldn't take but couldn't help myself from answering.

"I think she's ready for more," Chloe said after one such night. "You should have seen her last night, Max. She had a cloud of men around her."

"She told me about some tall guy who was really into her?"

"Yeah, there were a few of those, but I saw her really going at it with one of them in the back of the club. I swear he had his hand up under her dress."

"Really?" Heat sizzled across my face. She hadn't mentioned that.

"I don't know. It was dark and she didn't say anything on our way home other than that he was a good kisser." Chloe's laugh was cruel. "But the point is, I think she's ready for more. She's in town next Friday. I'm going to suggest you guys meet Greg and I for drinks."

"Just drinks?"

"Drinks and sex, I hope."

****

We were spending a quiet evening in, both of us working on our laptops at the dining table. *Study hall,* Katie called it. This had become the norm. When Mya went down, if we weren't busy getting caught up in the bedroom, we were busy catching up in our work. Katie was pouring over some audit reports when she paused, looked over at me, and asked the question I'd been waiting to hear for days.

"So Chloe asked if we wanted to meet her and Greg for drinks."

I replied with the question same question I'd given Chloe. "Just drinks, or...?"

I saw Katie's smile light up her eyes behind her glasses. "*Or,*" she said. "If you're up for it."

I had a brief, intense vision of Greg and Katie, their naked bodies bathed in shadow as they rutted in the dark. I took a deep, steadying breath. "Let's talk about that."

"Sure." Katie took off her glasses and batted her lashes. "What do you want to talk about?"

She went coy.

I went blunt. "Sex with other people."

"A familiar subject these days." She giggled.

I reached across the table and took her hands in mine. "Honey, are you going to be okay with me and Chloe?"

Katie expression tightened. "I think so."

I could read the rest of her thought: *it's not fair if I'm not.*

"I don't have to go there. I can just watch..." I hoped I sounded sincere. For the most part, I was, although I won't deny it, part of me (a very hard part of me) liked the idea of sex with Chloe.

"Really? You'd be okay with that?" she asked.

"This is about the two of us *together*, not our individual desires. I'm not going to do anything you're not comfortable with."

The tension ran out of her face. "And you're comfortable with me sleeping with Greg?"

"Little late in the game to be asking that, don't you think?"

Katie laughed. "I mean, *watching* me sleep with Greg."

"I can't wait for that."

****

"So here we are," Greg said as a server placed our drinks in front of us.

I'd decided on a double bourbon and Coke, needing something strong and direct to calm my frayed nerves.

"Here we are," I repeated.

Greg sat across from me, a beer before him and the same easy smile I'd noticed the first time I'd met him. We sat at the bar in the Azure Lounge, a small bar on the first floor of the boutique hotel, Azure. I checked my watch. Just past nine. We had the babysitter until around one a.m.—two if we needed to stretch it out. I couldn't decide if fours hours was too much time or too little.

It was really weird to be standing next to a guy who'd fucked my wife—Katie's *lover*. He didn't mention the encounter, he was too much a gentleman to do that, but I could see it in his eyes. The balance of power had shifted in the slightest of ways. We were no longer just a couple guys with a fetish for wife-watching. He had something on me, and by the end of the night, he'd have even more.

"How about a toast to you and Katie joining the club," Greg suggested, drawing me back to him. The two of us had come ahead of the women. That was part of the game.

I didn't feel like this was a celebratory kind of thing, but raised my glass anyway. I even managed to make a joke, even as I felt everything falling apart around me. "Do we get matching jackets?"

"It gets a little easier," Greg said. *Was I that obviously nervous?* "But not really." He laughed. "I mean, that's what keeps drawing us back, right? That thrill that sometimes feels like panic?"

"Yeah." I knew what he meant, but that wasn't quite it. Something else had me on edge, and that *something else* walked in at that moment with my wife.

Chloe was a bombshell—even more, she knew it. Katie had more natural beauty and grace than the blonde could ever have, but Chloe carried herself like a glamour model. She wore a short, yet loose black dress, cinched around her narrow waist by a glossy black belt, and tall, spindly heels elongated her diminutive size.

Katie walked in behind her, more dolled up than usual in a short black skirt and red blouse—not quite the wife and mother I woke up next to every day, but still familiar. Even if she weren't my wife—even if these two were strangers to me—I'd gravitate toward Katie and her authentic beauty.

And yet, when Greg turned to me and mouthed, *Here we go,* it was Chloe that I found myself approaching.

That was the game. Or a twist on the game. Instead of sitting back and watching them get picked up, we were role-playing—only it was the other man's wife that we were role-playing with.

"Buy you two a drink?" Greg asked.

I smiled at Chloe, falling into the wingman role. I wondered how many times the blonde played second fiddle to any woman.

"Please," Katie said. "I'll take a margarita."

"And you?" I asked the blonde. We shared a smile as we settled into our fake personas.

"I'll take the same. Tequila sounds fun."

We stayed around the bar, pairing off with each others' spouses much like we had over dinner a few weeks back. Only tonight, the pairings had the potential to go further than casual conversation.

"I really like your blouse," Greg said, his eyes sliding into the generous scoop of Katie's red top.

Chloe rolled her eyes and looked at me, whispering, "Do you have a better line?"

"You don't need me to tell you how good you look," I said. "But if you want, I can tell you that every guy in this room wishes they were me right now."

Chloe batted her lashes. "Not great, but better than his."

"Thanks for being generous," I said. "You two local? Or visiting?"

Pretending to be a stranger felt a little forced, but it was easier than it would have been with Katie since Chloe really *was* mostly a stranger.

"Local," she said. Her drink arrived and I handed it to her. "Katie and I are on a girls night out."

"I'm glad you picked this spot," I said.

As the drinks flowed, the role-play got easier. Chloe was easy to talk to, and after a while, I even managed to give her more attention than Katie and Greg, who seemed to be picking up right where they left off. At one point, Greg had her laughing harder than I'd seem her in a long while. Jealousy swam through my veins, washed to the furthest reaches of my body.

"She can't wait to fuck him again, you know," Chloe whispered, breaking role. "Isn't that exciting?"

Jealousy bloomed inside me. "And you're fine with that?"

"I get a little something out of it, too," she said, snuggling close enough to fill my nose with her heady perfume.

"Chloe...Katie and I talked about it, and—"

"She doesn't want you fooling around with me. I know. She told me."

"Then...?"

"You're okay with that arrangement? You're cool with her fucking other men, leaving you with nothing but scraps?"

I licked my lips, shooting a glance at Katie. She was deep in a conversation of her own with Greg, their heads close, their eyes locked.

"I am, if that's what she wants," I said, although Chloe's questions had rattled my confidence.

"So when Greg asks her to go up to the room he's reserved, and she agrees, you aren't going to feel even a little left out?" Chloe leaned close. "Because I can make you feel all warm and cozy again if you let me."

When she leaned back, I saw the question leave Greg's lips. *Want to go upstairs?*

Katie's eyes slid away from him reluctantly, resting on me. I gave her the little nod I hadn't been able to that first night the four of us had gone dancing and she was with that Latin hunk. She smiled, mouthed an *I love you*, and turned back to Greg.

Watching Katie leave with her hand in Greg's felt like the early stages of a sickness. Things were off, but not enough to stand up and take action. Greg slid his hand down her back, resting it on her ass, and looked back at us—whether at me or Chloe, I didn't know. Then they rounded the corner to the elevator lobby and were gone.

"How do you feel now?" Chloe said. Her hand touched the inside of my thigh, dangerously close to my erection.

"I'm good. Nothing new here." I could put on macho airs as much as the next guy.

"If you're talking about those two, that's *definitely* true."

"I'm really horny. Let's go."

She rose. I rose.

"To my room?" she asked.

"Chloe..."

"Or we could go to theirs. You can watch my Gregory rock Katie's world." Her hand finally found my crotch, throbbing and hard. "Is that what you want?"

Yes, but could I handle it? I stalled, groping for those other questions. "I thought Greg was the one who liked to watch?"

Chloe sat back and reached for her drink. "That's how it started. He played the nice little cuckold for almost a year before we discovered just how effective a bull he could be."

Cuckold. Bull. The words had my ears burning. I didn't like the idea of those roles, and how neatly I might fit into one of them.

"I think that since he understands what it's like to be on the receiving end so well, he knows exactly how to press buttons," Chloe said. "And it's awesome to watch him in action."

"And you're okay with him with other women?"

"Of course. I love it, in fact. I think it's awesome to know that my man still has it." She tucked a strand of blonde hair behind her hear. "I never understood jealous women. Just feels insecure to me."

That felt like a jab at Katie. I considered rising to defend, but realized that it confused me, too. After all, here I was down in the lobby, letting her play with someone else. For possibly the first time—or maybe just the first time that I noticed—resentment seeped into my fantasy.

"And besides," Chloe went on. "Sometimes, I get to join them. Those experiences definitely make everything else worthwhile. There's nothing like watching Greg fuck some married slut from behind as she eats me out."

For a moment, Katie became that *married slut*. "I wouldn't

hold your breath with her. She lived four years in a sorority without having a lesbian experience. I doubt you're going to get her to have one now."

"I bet she didn't play around with other guys back then, either, but she's doing it now. I've had so many firsts in my thirties." She slipped off her stool and pressed herself against me. "Would you believe I'd never had a threesome with two guys until just recently?"

"Thirties are the new twenties, huh?" I said.

Chloe nodded, choosing not to hear it as a joke. "I'm horny and need to get out of here. So we go to my room, or theirs. Your choice."

I rose beside her, discretely adjusting my erection. As much a temptation as Chloe was, this choice was easy. "Theirs."

****

Azure, being a boutique hotel, was only ten floors tall. The hotel room that Greg had reserved was on the tenth, and when the elevator lobby opened onto the floor, a short hall lead down to just four doors.

"Let me guess, yours is one of the others?" I said.

Chloe nodded. "Change your mind?"

"Keep dreaming."

"I always will." She led me down to the door at the far end, marked with an elegant 4. She paused, turning to me. "And Max, I almost always make my dreams come true."

With that, she slipped her keycard into the lock and opened the door to a hotel room as large as the first apartment Katie and I lived in.

I wasn't sure what to expect. Maybe Katie and Greg sitting on the couch, a bottle of wine open and their knees together? Maybe Katie straddling his lap as they made out, clothes loosened but still intact? Nothing like what I actually saw.

"Uh, uh, UH!" Katie's moans slammed into me like a careening bus.

"You like that, baby? You like how good my cock feels?" Greg's questions swam beneath Katie's moaning cacophony, driving her on like a rancher would a herd. "You missed it, didn't you?"

"Yesss...oh—fuck me. Fuck ME!"

And that was just what I heard. It was like stepping out of my life and onto the set of a porn film. Chloe drew me into the room as my eyes adjusted to the dim lighting. It was set up like a studio: sitting area and television to one side, dining area with table to the other, and beyond, two king sized beds, one of which was very much occupied.

Their clothes left a trail across the room. I imagined them tearing at each other as they tore them off. Katie's skirt and blouse were by the door. Her thong on the surface of the table. Her bra by the edge of the bed. And on the bed...

"Jesus Christ, you're sexy, baby." Greg stood at the edge, feet planted on the floor, knees bent. Katie was on her back with her legs over Greg's shoulder. Her ass hung off the edge of the mattress. He held her by the ankles as he plunged his cock in and out of her pussy. "Play with your tits. Squeeze them for me."

Katie did as told, scooping her full breasts in her hands. She pushed them together, pinching her nipples as she did.

"Looks like they didn't waste time." Chloe's whisper snapped me back into my body, and with it, all the confused and arousing sensations that came with it. "Come on, let's get a better look."

Greg was more impressive naked than clothed. Those initial impressions of a passive man fell away at the sight of his lean muscle, covered in a light sheen of sweat and light body hair. He saw us as we followed the trail of discarded clothing. He gave me a nod over his shoulder, squeezing Katie's ankles harder. I took a seat at the edge of the bed, my body stiff, my attention completely on the action before me.

Greg leaned into Katie, lifting her by the ankles off the mattress as he crashed down into her. He huffed with her thrust, fucking her as fast as she could take it. Katie's arms flew out to either side if her, fingers digging into the sheets and twisting for stability as her orgasm hit her like a tidal wave.

I felt dizzy, watching my wife completely lose it with another man. The air seemed thinner, like her climax had sucked oxygen from the room.

Chloe slipped up behind me. "He's not done yet. Far from it," she whispered.

Katie flopped back onto the bed, huffing and limp. With one leg still up over his shoulder, he set the other on the floor and leaned into her, giving her a slow, deep kiss. My gut churned as I watched her return it, her hand rake into the back of his curly hair. From that intimate position, he began to pump his cock again.

"Let's get more comfortable," Chloe said. She began to work open the buttons of my shirt. I didn't stop her. I barely even felt her there, fluttering behind me as she removed my clothing. "Very nice," she whispered as her hands caressed my bare upper body.

She kissed my neck. I tensed, my eyes darting to Katie's. My wife's were still closed, and as Chloe's lips touched down on my neck a second time, Katie released a sharp moan.

Chloe unbuckled my belt. Katie finally noticed us, the metal clank drawing her back from her hazy world of decadent sex. She looked up at me from the mattress, eyelids heavy, her sigh ending in a smile.

Greg followed her gaze, grinning at the sight of his wife undressed me. For a split second, our roles were reversed and Greg was the voyeur again, watching his wife get dirty. I felt a surge of testosterone course through me, unfamiliar but not unpleasant. I thought about turning back to Chloe and kissing her, about pushing her between my legs and making her service me as her husband watched.

Those thoughts were gone as quickly as they'd arrived, like people entering a room, realizing they weren't supposed to be there, and ducking out. It wasn't me, and more to the point, I couldn't overlook the fact that Chloe's husband had his cock buried in my wife's willing pussy.

"We got started a little before you," Greg said. His hips didn't stop their rise and fall over Katie.

"We noticed," Chloe replied. To Katie: "Mind if I help your husband get naked?"

Katie glanced at Chloe, then back at me. She looked calm, but I sensed turmoil behind her serene, well-fucked expression. She took a deep breath, whether to steel herself for what she was about to say, or because Greg's cock felt particularly good at that moment, I couldn't say.

"He looks like he needs help," she said. Her voice seemed to skip along the surface of a warm, glassy lake. "I don't mind."

Chloe pushed my pants and boxers down together. My cock

sprang free before she caught it in her hand. Her skin was warm and soft, her grip unfamiliar. I hadn't had another woman touch me there in forever and I didn't know how I felt about it now.

I tried to cast my memory back to my conversation with Katie about limits, but it was like casting into fog. Had we said anything about handjobs? Or just *no sex*? And if *no sex*, then what counted as sex here?

Chloe detached herself from behind me and slipped onto the floor. "Now I'm feeling way overdressed."

A moment later, her black dress was around her ankles and she was naked but for a little black thong. With narrower hips and smaller breasts, different than my wife, but no less attractive. I licked my lips as I took in the details: the diamond-tipped navel bar, the rose tattoo on her left hip, nipples jutting hard and prominent from high on her tits.

She tugged the thong down one hip and my eyes re-centered. Her panties had just enough material to cover her mound. It was a short trip before she flashed the top of her pink slit. I caught a glimpse of her clit, sitting beneath the bare mound I'd glimpsed in the limo, so long ago.

Chloe looked over her shoulder, where Greg and Katie had paused in their rutting. Both eyes were on the blonde. Chloe's nostrils flared. Her eyes shimmered under the attention. Enough teasing. She wiggled her hips one more time and lowered the panties down her long legs.

"Ah. Now that's better," she said.

Greg whispered something to Katie that I couldn't hear. My wife bit her lip, but didn't say anything. He began to fuck her again, slower than before. I caught a word here and there, but never a full thoughts: "...curious..." and "...with the flow..."

Chloe held her hand out to me, seeming much taller than her 5'2" frame. I didn't know what she expected if I took her hand. I hesitated, looking to Katie for guidance. Her eyes were closed as Greg continued to whisper to her.

"Come on," Chloe said, shaking her hand at me. "Let's get even closer."

My hand slid into hers. The distance to the other bed was only a few feet, but I felt like I was being led down a steep, spiraling stairwell. Everything was about to get more intense.

Katie felt my weight on the bed and looked at me, smiling. *Hi,* she seemed to say. *I'm glad you're here.*

Her green eyes dimmed a moment later as Greg drove into her. The reminder of where we are and what we were doing jolted through me. I watched Katie tip her head back, brow creased, nostrils flaring, as she enjoyed another man's cock—just inches away.

Instinctively, I dropped my hand to my erection. Chloe was already there. Before I could stop her, her wet mouth closed around me. I should have shut it down right there. The part of my brain that governed rational thought knew that I was crossing a line that Katie wouldn't be cool with. But the rest of me that was enjoying the slick warmth of Chloe's mouth didn't care.

So I turned to Katie and kissed her hard, and when she responded with a moan into my mouth, I told myself that this was okay.

Katie broke the kiss as another orgasm welled up inside her. She kept her eyes open as long as she could, keeping the connection between us. I could practically see her consciousness reduced to a single point of pure bliss. At the same moment, Chloe swallowed my cock into her throat. My breath caught. I came with Katie, erupting inside another woman's mouth for the first time in forever.

In the come down, I felt guilt course through me like pollution. Did Katie know what Chloe had just done—what I'd let Chloe do to me?

"Oh, fuck, baby," Greg moaned.

Looking down the length of Katie's still heaving body, I discovered that Chloe hadn't remained idle. She'd unsheathed Greg's cock from its latex shielding and stuffed him down her throat, bobbing fast. I'd somehow blocked out how large he was from our experience in the limo.

For the first time since I'd opened myself to the possibility of Katie being with this couple, I felt intimidated.

Chloe fondled Greg's balls as she blew him, overwhelming his impressive willpower. With a loud grunt, his eyes fluttered shut and he filled the blonde's mouth with her second helping of cum that night.

This time, though, she didn't swallow. Instead, she crawled up between Katie and I, touched my wife's face, and kissed her hard. Katie's eyes shot wide, but before she could stop the kiss, the blonde filled her mouth with tongue and cum and saliva.

Katie's resistance fell away. Her eyes fluttered shut as she gave herself to the Sapphic kiss—her first real kiss with another woman. My cock found its second wind. I shimmied up to the headboard, reclining into the mountain of pillows.

Greg's eyes met me from the other side of the women. He grinned and nodded, stroking his own cock back to life. Insecurity wriggled in my belly at his size—Katie had never complained about my size, but how could I compete with that?

"Oh, God," Katie groaned, drawing my attention back to them. Chloe had dropped an arm down my wife's body, her fingers following the narrow stripe of auburn hair. Katie tightened as the other woman danced her fingertips along her clit, her moan caught, then quickly released.

Chloe whispered something in Katie's ear before placing kisses along her neck. I leaned closer, catching the last of it.

"...so sexy. You're so wet. You're going to love this next part."

Chloe's lips dribbled lower, her mouth finding Katie's breasts, nipples swollen and ready to be sucked. Chloe obliged her, swirling her tongue across my wife's pale peaks as she continued to work her fingers along Katie's pussy.

As Chloe switched breasts, she looked up at Greg, a quick burst of silent communication passing between them. He got the message and crawled up closer to Katie's face, cock in hand.

Katie felt him there, her eyes locking onto his thick dick. She reached for it with greed, tugging it closer. Craning her neck, she took it into her mouth and sucked it. I could almost see the logic in her head: as much as she loved the way Chloe was making her feel, she loved men first, and sucking cock reminded her of that.

But when Chloe's mouth replaced her fingers between Katie's legs, all logic vaporized under the crushing pleasure. She moaned around Greg's member, but he wouldn't release her. He held himself inside her as she worked through the micro-orgasm. Her body arched, her nostrils flared. She lifted a leg onto Chloe's back, then set it back down and opened her legs wider.

It was something I'd never thought I'd see in a million years: my wife filled at both ends, a cock in her mouth and a woman's tongue in her pussy. It was so incongruous with my reality that I wouldn't have believed it if I wasn't here, witnessing it with my own eyes. I rode so close to the edge of my own orgasm that I didn't dare even touch my cock. I just watched, drinking in the debauchery.

Greg finally pulled out when Katie's world boiled over. Chloe had both hands working her, in addition to her tongue. There was nowhere for my wife to hide from the fire. She bowed backwards, tits in her hands, nipples between her fingers, and released a breathy scream.

I wondered if the walls were soundproofed. If not, I wondered if we'd get complaints. If someone came to the door, how would we explain it?

They were good questions to think about. Easier ones than those prompted by what I'd just witnessed. Definitely easier than the squirming concern I felt as Katie crawled over to Greg and took him back into her mouth.

"Jesus, Katie, you do that so well, but you know what would feel even better?" He urged her up into his lap, and she took the hint. It was Katie who reached between her legs, took hold of his cock, and positioned it against her. "Do it," he urged.

Before she lowered herself, she looked across his broad shoulders, finding me at the head of the bed. Our eyes locked. A smile turned up the corners of her mouth. And like that, I felt my insecurities fall away.

"Uh, fuck!" Katie's emoted the words as much as she said them, her body crying out as much as her breath. Her eyelids hung low, but behind them, she kept her eyes on me. She might have been with Greg physically, but her mind was with me.

Like all poignant moments go, this one was gone in an instant. We shared it, it was logged into the story of us, and then we moved on. Or, in this case, Chloe moved us on.

"Don't worry," she said, suddenly before me. Her petite frame blocked out the other couple, although I could still hear their wet union and the sharp gasps of fucking. "He's clean."

Chloe's words lacked meaning at first, like she'd spoken them in another language. Understanding descended like a tornado, striking with dizzying fury.

Don't worry, he's clean. Greg wasn't wearing a condom. I should have been incensed. It should have been a mood killer. Instead, my heart jumped into overdrive, beating so hard I felt it in the throb of my cock.

"I'm clean, too," Chloe said. "*Very* clean..."

A heartbeat later, I felt her pussy slide along my length, the bare skin of her sex reinforcing the double entendre.

It would have been so easy to just fuck her. I wouldn't have had to do a thing—just lie back and let her take me. Imagining how good her pussy would feel—the warm tightness of her new embrace—was so real that I panicked for a moment that it was.

Reality snapped back. Chloe was there, blue irises reflecting the warm light of the bedside lamp like an ocean on fire. She danced her bald sex along my length one more time, her slippery femininity caressing the sensitive underside, all the way down to my balls, then back again.

She moved in for the kill. My breath caught. It would feel so good. So, so fucking good. But—

"I can't." I took hold of Chloe's shoulders and lifted her off and away. "I can't."

And I didn't need to, I didn't say.

Chloe looked stunned. I wondered if she'd ever been rejected like this. As she stared at me, an incredulous look marring her pretty features, I actually felt bad for her. She'd gone into this night with a set of expectations, just like Katie and I; hers were just different.

"Oh, fuck me." Katie's cries refocused us. "Fuck ME!"

"You like that, don't you, baby." Greg egged her on. "You like getting some strange."

"Ah, fuck...me!"

"Your pussy is unbelievable. So tight..."

Chloe slipped away from me, drawn to Katie and Greg's rutting bodies. She flashed me a withering look, one that said, *You had your chance.*

Sliding in behind Katie, Chloe reached around and cupped my wife's full tits in her hands, kissing the side of her neck.

"You love how good he feels, don't you?" Chloe whispered, loud enough for me to hear. She glanced over at me. "How full he feels, sliding in and out of you. He can hit spots that you'd forgotten about."

Katie's only answer was a groan. Chloe laid kisses along her neck as her hands continued to caress her breasts.

"God, Katie, you're unbelievably hot." Chloe kissed along Katie's jaw, rising up onto her haunches. "I can't wait to eat his cum out of that pretty pussy of yours."

Greg planted his hands on the meat of Katie's ass, lifted her up, and held her steady as he pounded her from beneath. Chloe tipped her head back and drove her tongue into Katie's mouth.

It was too much for my wife. Sandwiched between the couple, she tore her mouth away from Chloe, threw her head back against the blonde's shoulder, and shuddered.

Chloe met her husband's gaze and nodded. "Do it, baby. Fill

this slut with your cum so I can lick it out of her."

Greg grunted, his cock a jackhammer flipped upside down. "Chloe, baby, you're such a dirty whore."

Chloe winked at him, took a hand off Katie's tits, and touched his face.

The exchange was bizarrely relatable. I'd never call Katie a dirty whore, just as Katie and I would never bond over tag-teaming someone else's wife, but I could relate to their intimacy, as profound as it was unconventional.

I yearned to touch Katie again, to share that moment. I didn't get my chance immediately, though. Chloe seemed determined to deliver on her promises.

Greg set Katie onto her back as she breathed through the last of her climax. His cock slid free, flaccid and coated in a cocktail of their combined juices. I caught a flash of Katie's pussy, the trail of another man's cum glossy in the low light of the room, before Chloe climbed over her.

As if to prove that I could still be shocked, Chloe swung her legs over Katie's head as she dipped between my wife's thighs, forming a one-sided sixty-nine.

Greg dragged himself off the bed and flopped into the desk chair. He rested his chin on an elbow and grinned over at me before encouraging my wife to do the unthinkable. "Go on, Katie. Don't be shy. We know you're curious."

Chloe lowered her hips until her pussy was just an inch away from Katie's mouth. Katie rocked her head back and searched for me wide-eyed. She licked her lips, more from nerves than anything salacious.

I nodded, encouraging, although still not believing.

Katie took a deep breath, closed her eyes, and ran her tongue tentatively along Chloe's swollen labia. The blonde had been watching over her shoulder. As soon as she felt Katie's touch, though, she dropped her hips and smothered Katie's with her bare shaven femininity. And with that done, her attention returned to fully to slurping Greg's cum from Katie.

I could not believe my eyes. No way was this happening. No way was this not a dream. Yet no matter how many times I blinked or rubbed my eyes, Katie was still splayed out before me, sixty-nining another woman like she'd done it all her life.

"Yeah, Kates. Right there. That feels...so good." Chloe gnawed her lower lip, looking back down her body as she reveled at Katie's ministrations.

Katie wasn't having it. She hooked her leg over Chloe's head and pulled her back to her cunt. Her assertiveness sent a thrill through me. This wasn't for show. She was as into the sex as I was watching it.

"Go on, Max," Greg said. He was in full voyeur mode. "Fuck Chloe. She wants it. You want it. What's stopping you?"

Katie didn't seem to hear—maybe she didn't with the blonde's thighs closed around her.

It would have been easy to slide into her. I was hard enough. Chloe was wet enough. But no.

"They look like they're doing a pretty good job on their own."

I half expected Greg to rise out of the chair, cock once again hard, and demonstrate how *a man* did it. Instead, he shrugged and let it go. "It's fun to watch, too. For sure."

The Greg from our first meeting was back. The one who'd hunched alone at the end of the bar as his wife flirted with strangers. The one that I didn't understand at the time, but now related to.

They drew frenzied energy from the other's gasps and moans, the sexiest duet I'd ever heard.

They came together (as far as I could tell). Their cries crashed as one, their bodies a tangle of slender arms and soft flesh.

Chloe rolled free, her tight body beaded with sweat. Katie put a hand on her forehead and sighed. "Wow..."

Chloe shifted around until she faced the same direction as my wife. "Was it as good as your fantasies?"

"I..."

My ears perked up. Would she deny having the fantasy? Or confirm it, having never admitted it.

"...yeah. Better. I mean, I never really thought about it much, but...yeah."

Chloe gave Katie a tender, yet passionate kiss. "I hope you think about it a lot more after tonight."

I loved that Katie still managed to blush, despite everything that had happened. She sat up and glanced at the clock. "Wow, it's late. We need to get back."

Chloe's eyes flittered down to my erection, as if to say, *You should have fucked me when you had the chance.* Instead, she said, "Tonight was fun. We should do it again sometime soon."

Neither Katie nor I acknowledged it as we got dressed. The other couple pulled on robes, apparently intending to stay the night. My chest tightened as Greg pulled Katie close and kissed her goodbye. Then Chloe distracted me with a kiss of her own.

"I'll be in touch," Chloe said. "Have a safe ride home."

Neither Katie nor I said a word on our way down to the parking garage. I tried to gather my thoughts, but it was like trying to rake leaves in a windstorm. I'd watched her fuck another man. Finally. But it hadn't been the first man she'd fucked. Would this be the last time? Or would she want more?

Inside the quiet cab of our car, the silence was deafening. I cranked the engine but didn't immediately pull out of the parking spot.

Next to me, Katie put a hand on my leg. Her face looked sharper, lit only by the fluorescent lights of the parking garage. "I love you," she said. Then: "Are we okay?"

How could such a complex question be boiled down into one three-word yes-or-no question? And yet I had an answer for it. "Yeah. We are."

Her hand traveled up my thigh as a smile formed. I wasn't erect anymore, but I wasn't exactly flaccid, either. "Sorry we left you frustrated there at the end."

"It's okay."

"No," she said, tucking her hair back behind her ear. "It's not."

She dropped her head into my lap, unzipped me, and fished my stiffening member free. As she took me into her mouth and I quickly scanned the empty parking lot for people, I wondered when that dream-like feeling would fade. I watched Katie's auburn hair bob in my lap, her tongue doing wild things to my cock, and thought for the last time that night, *Who is this woman who looks so much like my wife?*

CHAPTER 10

"Yes, I understand...yes, I can do that, but—" Katie made a face, but kept listening to whatever was being said on the other end of the phone.

"Uh, huh...right."

We hadn't even crawled out of bed. It was ten in the morning. I couldn't remember the last time we'd *both* slept in so late, yet after last night's marathon sex session with Chloe and Greg, we both needed it.

We'd come home around 2, apologized to the babysitter, then crashed. Neither of us were ready to talk about what had happened beyond simple reassurances. The talk would come—later this morning, I was hoping—and all would be all right. Only, it didn't seem to be playing out that way.

"Okay, I'm on my way." Katie sounded annoyed at whoever had called her so "early" on a Saturday morning. "Yes, I understand."

She jammed her thumb against the End button and tossed it

down to the foot of the bed. Flopping onto her back, she blew out a loud sigh and shook her head. "I need to get to the airport."

"What?" That wasn't what I was expecting. "When? Why?"

Her snort was one of exasperation. "I need to get on an airplane that's leaving in two hours. I'm not sure that's even possible. There's apparently some crisis in our Hong Kong office. Apparently I'm needed there."

"Hong Kong?" She'd been traveling a lot, but that was by far the most distant she'd been.

"It gets worse. They need me there for three weeks."

"Three weeks? That's a long time."

She looked guilty. "At least I won't miss the opening of the speakeasy?"

I still hadn't told her the name I'd come up with, and somehow I'd managed to keep it a secret despite the menus and promos being created. I wanted the place to be my gift to her. "It's still so long. And…"

"What?" she asked.

"It's going to sound silly, but I was kind of looking forward to spending a little time, just you and me."

Katie touched my face. "I'll see what I can do to get back. Trust me, I'm not a fan of this, either." She rolled out of bed, grabbed her robe from the bathroom, and began packing. "I'm going to do my best to get home earlier. Can you go wake Mya up and get her ready?"

****

I could handle being a single dad for three weeks. I could even handle being a single dad for three weeks while putting the finishing touches on my bar opening. The nanny, Eleanor, helped. So did my parents and Nadia.

Katie being out of the country actually made a few things easier, too, like being able to review menus with *The Katherine* letterpressed onto them, or having a phone conversation without having to call the bar *the speakeasy*.

The hardest part wasn't even the void of sex—although after these last few months of fucking like newlyweds, the lack of sexual relief wasn't the easiest thing to deal with, either.

No, the hardest thing was not having Katie with me. My best friend. My companion. I missed being able to talk to her about how her day was. Or relate a crazy story I'd heard from a drunk at the bar. Or wake up in the middle of the night and know that she was at my side, peacefully asleep.

We did end up having that post-swing conversation, only about a day delayed and over the phone. It was my morning, her night, and she'd been traveling for nearly 15 hours. Not ideal circumstances, but for me, it couldn't wait anymore.

"How are you feeling?" I said. "About our night with Greg and Chloe?"

"Gosh, from where I am now, that feels like ages ago." Her laugh had more sigh behind it than exhilaration. "I had fun. You?"

It was so much harder to have this talk without looking into each other's eyes. Was this a test or a genuine question? I took it as the latter. "Yeah, it was fun. A lot of fun."

"You got a little closer to Chloe, I noticed."

Again, I wished I could see her face. Instead, I was forced to sift through her tone in search of jealousy. "I'm sorry about that. I didn't—"

"Relax, honey. Everything was happening all at once. A lot of unplanned things happened."

The image of Chloe and Katie sixty-nining was suddenly all I could think about. "Yeah. I thought you told me you weren't curious about that."

"I wasn't...until I was." Now the exhilaration was there, although only just so.

"And now?"

"I'd be lying if I told you that wasn't fun, too. I guess I just never thought about it seriously."

My mind was blown. But this wasn't why I'd started this conversation.

"So what next?" I said.

"Are you asking whether I'm going to start *exploring my sexuality*? Because I'm perfectly happy with my sexuality as it is."

"No, I mean...about Greg and Chloe."

"How about we just play it by ear? Right now, I need to get through these next three weeks—as do you. When all this craziness has died down, we can figure the other stuff out."

I laughed. "Katie Callahan, moving forward without a plan?"

"Well, it's not like you can say it's the most shocking thing I've done recently."

We did our solid best to have conversations like that every day, but every day, the conversations got a little shorter and a little more abstract. Even from the other side of the globe and on her mobile phone, her voice came through crystal clear. The *I love yous* and the *I miss yous* could have been coming from the next room over. But they weren't, and after two weeks and with the bar's grand opening less than a month away, everything just got more and more academic.

"Everything's set for opening night. Just need to finalize the VIP list..." Nadia was talking, clipboard in hand, but I barely heard her. I was too busy missing Katie.

"Hey, hey!" Nadia said, snapping her fingers. "Earth to Max, you there? I need you with me. Just a few more weeks now, and you can go back to La-La Land."

It would be a shame losing her as the manager of Callahan 2, but I needed her operating my newest bar. The speakeasy would be a tricky thing to make popular: almost hidden from the outside, small on the inside, reservations required on peak nights, and a dress code right out of the 1920s. My hope was that all those things would create a buzz that would be irresistible for the young hipsters of the city.

"Sorry, sorry. I'm here. What were we talking about?"

"VIPs. I need you to look over this list and let me know if you have a problem with any of them."

Nadia handed me the clipboard and I distractedly reviewed the names. We'd decided at the last minute to invite the rich socialites of the city to this event. It was Nadia's idea, actually, but it was a good one. People would keep coming back on the off chance that they'd spot one of the B-list celebrities.

I recognized most of the names, but was beginning to wonder why Nadia thought I'd have a problem with any of them. Until I came upon two. I looked up at her. "Have the invites gone out?"

The brunette shook her head. "Course not. That's why I'm asking you to look, but don't take too long...we only have a few days left." She craned her neck to see the list. "See someone I should nix?"

I glanced back at the names. *Greg and Chloe Reynolds.* Of course their names would be on here. They were young and rich socialites. And really, I had no reason to protest them. It's just…I didn't think I wanted them in this part of my world.

"Um, no." I forced a smile. I was being silly.

Nadia looked at me funny. "Everything okay with you?"

Could I talk to her about this? Tell her about the crazy sex adventure that Katie and I were on? How she'd slept with another man, not once, but twice, or how she went out dancing with the man's wife and made out with other guys?

"I just miss Katie is all. It's crazy. How quickly it all goes. We've been together for nine years, but she's gone not even a two weeks and I start forgetting her?"

Nadia set her pen down on the scheduling notebook and reached for my hands. "You're not forgetting her. It's just the way you deal with missing her. And it's natural."

Nadia's wedding and engagement rings caught in the light, a large diamond encased in warm gold. Her wedding felt like ages ago, and as I drew up a mental timeline, I realized it had been over a year since she'd married John.

"How do you and John deal with it? Living apart. Here I am, crying about a couple weeks, and he's been working in New York since the restructuring."

Nadia pulled her hands away and stared at me like she had a secret. "It's not the best arrangement, but we're dealing with it."

Now it was my turn to probe. "What?"

"John and I have an…understanding."

I blinked. This was unexpected. Even with everything I knew about the young woman, I didn't expect *this*. "You're swingers?"

Nadia blushed beneath her deep tan. "I don't know that that's what we'd call it. More like an open relationship, I guess."

I ran my hand across my scalp as I tried to put it all together. Here I was, struggling with my own issues with an open relationship, when my right hand man (or woman) was living the life right beside me.

"You're not going to fire me, are you?" I'd never seen Nadia nervous, and when I looked up at her, I saw that her question was more of a tease than one of serious concern. "I could arrange another viewing for you if it would save my job."

That moment from three years returned in a flash, Nadia sprawled face down on the bar as some stud fucked her hard.

"You knew I was watching?"

Nadia laughed. "Yeah. It made is so much hotter. I probably wouldn't have gone that far if I didn't see you hiding there."

"I'm sorry."

Nadia shook her head. "Don't apologize. Like I said, it was hot. I like being watched."

"I thought marriage would mellow you out."

"Is that what it's supposed to do? Because in my experience, it's been the opposite."

I tried to imagine John, quiet John, acting like Greg—or even me, for that matter. It didn't gel, but then again, people probably wouldn't suspect that I'd get off on something as kinky as watching my wife in a threesome with another couple.

"Yeah, definitely doesn't have to."

After a relaxed silence, Nadia asked, "You and Katie are alright, right?"

The question triggered something uneasy in my belly. "Yeah.

Why?"

Nadia shook her head. "No real reason. Just wondering."

I started to ask her to elaborate, then spotted Chloe settle in at the bar. It was the first time I'd seen her since our crazy night together, and while that should have made me feel at ease with her, I felt everything but.

I pushed out of my seat. "Excuse me for a second, will you?"

Nadia nodded, going back to her books as walked toward Chloe. It felt like walking up to a live grenade.

"Hey, stranger," the now-familiar blonde greeted as I moved behind the bar. This afternoon, she was wearing skintight jeans and a tunic shirt that she'd belted to emphasize her slender build. Her skinny style jeans were tucked into a pair of slouchy brown boots and her pale hair hung short and free around her pretty face.

"Hey yourself," I said. "The usual?"

"You look great, as usual," I said.

She stretched, the tunic pulled tight enough to outline her bra. I looked, just as she'd intended.

"Well I hope so. Spent the whole day getting beauty treatments. You know how it is."

I didn't, but nodded anyway. Now that she mentioned it, her face glowed.

"So what brings you here this afternoon?" Tuesdays were always pretty dead. 4 o'clock on a Tuesday meant her presence doubled the number of paying patrons.

"Looking for you," she winked as I set her vodka tonic down. "You fixing yourself one?"

Chloe was synonymous with vice in my head, and she continued to live up to that reputation. I didn't see a problem with indulging her this time, so I fixed myself a drink.

"What's the occasion?" I raised my glass.

Her eyes met mine, smoky and ringed in dark eyeliner. Her response was husky, offered with a half-smile. "How about: to something forbidden."

"Such as?"

She tipped her lowball against mine, a smile consuming her face before she replied. "Our spouses fucking on the other side of the globe."

I wasn't sure what dropped faster, my jaw or my stomach. Both fell like lead. "What?"

Chloe checked her watch. "They're probably done by now. It's pretty late there, but maybe not. They both seemed pretty into it last time we got together."

"What are you talking about?" I understood the words, but they didn't make sense. "Katie's in Hong Kong..."

"So's Greg. They had dinner tonight. Or last night. Or whatever." She pulled her phone from her purse. "Here."

On her phone was a self-portrait of Greg and Katie. They looked like they were sitting in a rickshaw with the vibrant lights of Hong Kong smeared behind them. Even bundled up as she was in a puffy winter coat and a hat, Katie's beauty shined through. Greg, beside her, had one arm around her shoulders and the other held out to hold the camera.

My insides sizzled with jealousy.

"He was out there for business and looked her up."

Something about that situation didn't sit well with me. "What a coincidence," I said flatly.

"Hey, he's a financier. He goes where he wants. I'm not saying that Katie being alone in a foreign city *didn't* factor into it, but I didn't ask."

"And you don't have a problem with that?" I pointed at her phone.

Chloe reached across the bar and slid her fingers over mine. "Oh, I'm broken up about it. I was hoping you'd help me forget."

She didn't look broken up at all. She *looked* like a fox eyeing a sleeping hen.

I pulled away. "I don't think you understand, Chloe. You and I? We're not going to happen. I think you're sexy. If I was single, I'd be all over you without a second thought."

Although maybe not. There was something sinister about her, hiding beneath her vanilla scented perfume.

"But I'm with someone else now—"

"Someone who's cheating on you right now," Chloe hissed. "Someone who's naked in bed with my husband. Right now. And you know what? I bet she doesn't tell you tomorrow."

The word *cheat* rang like a bell. "No..."

Chloe rose out of her seat and downed her drink. "I'll call you tomorrow after I talk to Greg. We'll compare notes. Then we'll talk."

She sauntered out. I watched her the whole way.

"What was that all about?" Nadia asked once Chloe was gone.

I wondered how much she'd heard. Chloe and I had been speaking in hushed tones, but the bar was still empty.

"Nothing. I..."

Was Katie cheating on me? Was this the first time? I looked at Nadia—John's husband—who had an *understanding*.

"Has anything ever happened between Katie and John? Like on one of their trips?"

Nadia looked taken aback. "Anything like…?"

"Did they ever have sex? Please be honest, Nadia. I need to know."

"Are you kidding me? Really? Katie? She'd never do anything like that. Ever. She loves you too much and she's just not that way. And even if she was, John would never go there. Too complicated, what with you being my boss and all."

I nodded, still not convinced. I thought about Katie's confession so long ago, about the kiss she had with a young man in New York. John was on that trip.

"I think they may have kissed. A long time ago."

Nadia shook her head, and at first I thought it was out of anger. A moment later, I realized it was something else. "They didn't. Did Katie say that?"

"No."

"Then you're just being irrational and jealous—that's not like you, Maxwell Callahan! But trust me, if they had, I would have heard all about it. John's had a thing for your wife forever."

"Maybe he didn't want to tell you," I offered.

"But Max, why would he lie? He tells me a lot worse than just that a kiss."

"I don't know." I really didn't.

"Max." She pulled out her phone and fired it off to John.

–have you ever kissed katherine callahan? now, before we met, or ever?

His reply came a moment later.

–i wish. why?

"See? So tell me, Max, why would she make that up?"

"Now that's a long story."

"We've got all afternoon…"

I didn't tell her all the details, although I told her most. I told her about my first meeting with Greg and Chloe, about Nadia's wedding and how I'd gotten jealous of John's gay cousin (which drew a big laugh from Nadia). I told her about Halloween, about Greg and last week at Azure.

Throughout, though, I talked about my excitement and my fear, and how one was almost never without the other.

And in the end, it was cathartic. I felt the way I had after walking out of Confession when I was a boy: the realities were still all there, but now they weren't so bottled up anymore.

"Wow," Nadia said at the end. "I had no idea you had all that hiding in your closet, Max. We need to close early and get out of here. We've got to make up for lost time."

"But now she's with Greg."

Nadia said the thing that had been tickling the back of my brain for a while: "I don't trust those two."

"Yeah."

Nadia pressed. "How did they even know she was even in Hong Kong?"

"I don't know. Maybe he's got some contact in the firm?"

She tapped her lips. "Maybe… Whatever the case, I don't trust them. That woman who walked out of here isn't the type of woman who is told no, and you've been telling her no since you first met. Be careful, Max."

"Thanks for the warning. And thanks for listening, too. I needed to get that off my chest."

"I can help you get all kinds of things off your chest," she said with a wink. "But until you clear that with your wife, I'll continue to dream."

****

The elation of being able to share my experiences with someone lasted about an hour. Then the reality of the situation came crashing down around me. Katie had taken another man into her bed behind my back. Even if she confessed tomorrow, that fact would remain.

And if she didn't? That left the door open to all kinds of other questions. Was this the first time she'd fooled around with another man? How could I trust her again?

I recalled my conversation with Greg—a conversation that felt like a lifetime ago, but was only about a month. Was I like him? Was it the possibility of her being bad that turned me on? I couldn't deny that part of this did turn me on. Thing was, the *not knowing* part ruined me. The deception. The loss of trust. I could handle Katie getting physical with another man—I knew that without a doubt now. I could handle it whether I was there or not. But I needed to know about it. I *had* to know about it.

I wanted to call. A half dozen times, I had her number drawn up. All I had to do was press send. But I couldn't bring myself to do that. I imagined the phone ringing on the nightstand by the bed as she moaned beneath Greg's pumping body. What if she answered then? How fucking humiliating would that be?

The worst part was that a small piece of me got excited by that prospect. But it was small, and getting smaller by the minute. Like the patrons who'd be flooding into The Katherine in just three weeks, I only wanted the illusion of something forbidden. I wasn't Chloe or Greg. I didn't actually want it.

"Hey hon, how are you?" I called Katie the next morning after a fitful night's sleep. It was already her evening. I wondered what she was up to. Was he there? Was she getting ready to go out with him?

"I'm good. How are you?"

"I'm good." How awkward was this? I took a deep breath. Time to get into the uncomfortable details, the ones that governed our future. The talk that wasn't The Talk. "So how was your day?"

"It was an interesting one, that's for sure." She sounded exhausted.

"Want to tell me about it?"

"Greg showed up yesterday."

That thing that I'd been so worried she wouldn't tell? There is was, offered without effort. All that bottled apprehension released with Katie's tired admission. And for the first time since Chloe had walked out of my bar, I began to wonder if there was anything to admit. How quickly I'd jumped to her spoon-fed conclusion.

"That's an odd coincidence."

Katie sounded reenergized. "Isn't it?"

"You don't think it was?"

"He says he's here to close a big deal, but I'm not sure what to think. I'm still working that out."

"Okay. Keep me posted." Then the obsessed part of me had to go and ruin a perfectly good conversation. "So he showed up yesterday, huh?"

I could practically see Katie's eyes roll in her tone. "Max, not tonight. It's been a long day."

"I'm sorry. Had to ask."

"You know I wouldn't do that, right? Not without you here."

"You did it before, when I wasn't there," I said.

"That was different. We talked about it first. You'd really be okay if something had happened?"

"No, you're right. Before was different. It's just…" I thought about telling her about Chloe's visit, the picture, and the blonde's suggestion. Instead, I kept all that to myself. "I don't know, I miss you. I can't wait for you to get home."

"Well, looks like I may be finishing up here early. I should be back by the weekend."

"Oh, thank God."

"Night, Max. Or good morning. Or whatever it is there."

"Good night and good morning to you, Katie. Bye."

I pulled myself out of bed and took a shower, feeling like a new man. Katie hadn't slept with Greg. She hadn't cheated on me. What was most disturbing was how quickly I'd jumped to that conclusion. I puzzled through that as I pretended to read the news on my iPad.

"Good morning, sleepyhead," I said from the door to our daughter's room.

"Good *morning*," she croaked, her voice still full of sleep. "Where's Mommy?"

She'd asked the same question every morning since Katie had flown away. This time, when I answered, I felt the same rush of impatience for my wife's return that Mya must have felt every day. "She's away right now, but she'll be back."

"She's on a trip," Mya confirmed. Her voice was so pure. When she spoke, everything was matter-of-fact. It was reassuring. "She'll be back soon."

"She will. Very soon. And this time, we're not going to let her leave."

CHAPTER 11

When Chloe called later that day, I answered, resolute in my confidence. Oh, how easy she picked it apart.

"So you two talked?"

"Yeah, talked to Katie this morning. She even mentioned Greg, so there. You were wrong."

Something about the tenor of Chloe's laugh was pure evil. "I didn't say she wouldn't mention Greg. I said she wouldn't mention them fucking. She didn't, did she?"

"Because they didn't."

"Did you ask?"

It was so satisfying to answer that one. "I did, actually. We talked a little about it. She said that she'd never do that without checking with me first."

"Huh. Well, seems we got very different stories from our spouses!"

This was absurd. I knew where my trust lay, and it wasn't in the woman on the other and of the phone. And yet, I kept listening anyway.

"Want to know what I heard?" she asked. When I didn't reply, she took it as an indicator to continue. "They had a great dinner together, just talking then—apparently they have a lot in common. Maybe it's *me* who should be worried. They took a pedicab tour around Hong Kong before heading back to your wife's hotel. She actually invited him up, although Greg swears they were both just going up for a night cap—"

"This is bullshit, Chloe. You can stop now."

"But I'm just getting to the good stuff. Apparently your Katie had an awesome view of the city. Did you know that? Something like the 66th floor?"

I did remember her mentioning that a few times, but anyone with a small amount of investigative skills could have learned that. "I'm still not buying it."

"Okay, well, once they were up there, they couldn't really keep their hands off each other. They'd already crossed that barrier… what? Two times already, right? That's the logic that Katie actually used, so Greg said. After that…well, they didn't get much sleep that night. And from what I'm gathering, not much tonight, either."

I thought about how tired Katie had sounded on the phone. Doubt took hold, but stubbornness spoke.

"Bullshit, Chloe. Goodbye."

I hung up before she could fill my head with anymore…lies.

****

I thought about telling Nadia, but after that initial confession,

I felt ashamed to share Katie's infidelity. Nadia and John had things figured out. I'd come off like a novice to this game. Stupidly, I let that affect my judgment.

Katie actually finished up her project in Hong Kong that night, while I slept. The next phone call I got was from her during my morning, telling me that she was flying out. Any further discussion would have to wait until she arrived home.

The meeting at the airport was glorious, despite any doubts or reservations I had. Mya ran into Katie's arms. There were tearful *hellos* and *welcome homes*. No one could stop smiling the entire drive back, or through the dinner out.

We ate at Callahan 2 because it was on the way home and I knew we wouldn't have to fight to get a table on a Friday night. The bar scene was just beginning to pick up, but it would be a few more hours before the dining area was cleared to make way for the true money-maker of the evening.

Nadia was on duty when arrived and greeted us with a hearty hello.

"Katie, I feel like I haven't seen you in ages," Nadia said after hugging my wife.

"Since the holiday party, right?"

"Has it been that long? That's crazy. Next time John's in town, the four of us should get together for drinks."

I nearly choked at the implication of that, but Nadia didn't take her eyes off my wife.

"That would be great. How's John doing in New York?"

"Being lonely. Don't tell anyone, but he's looking to start up his own accounting firm. Something small and, more importantly, back here."

"Well, tell him if he's looking for another accountant, I can send my resume over." Katie laughed. "All this travel is killing me. I don't know how you and John do it."

This time, Nadia glanced at me before swinging her eyes down to Mya. "We don't have a little one, first of all. Otherwise, we make it work."

"That's all we can do," Katie agreed.

The dynamic was so different now between them. Was that just time? Marriage? Katie and I dabbling in the world of swinging? Probably the latter more than anything else.

"I think I'm going to have the fish and chips," Katie announced, closing her menu.

"So much fried food. How unlike you."

"I know, but I need to get Hong Kong out of my system, and I figure fish and chips is about as far from Hong Kong as you can get."

Get it out of your system? But why? "Something happen you want to talk about?"

Did Katie's eyes dart to Mya? Or was I being paranoid?

"Actually, yeah, I do. But first, let's order."

Here's the thing I love so much about Katie. She comes at things logically, matter-of-factly. When she sees a problem, she immediately sets about solving it. Me, I can sometimes wallow a little, I'll admit, and that's gotten me into trouble. I'd begun to wallow here, but as soon as the orders were in, Katie pulled me out of that.

"I think Greg—or at least his company—is up to something involving his Far East contracts."

That was not what I was expecting to hear. "Yeah?"

"Yeah. And here's the thing: I think it involves my firm." Our pints arrived, she took a sip, and quickly went on. "I don't know the extent of it, but it's just too much of a coincidence that this crisis comes up and then Greg shows up right after. And while he wasn't in any of the meetings I was with, I'm pretty sure he's meeting with a lot of the same companies. And he's still over there."

"Maybe he came over to seduce you."

Katie laughed it away like that was a total impossibility. The seed of doubt Chloe had sown wondered if that was good acting.

"That's a pretty pricey seduction, don't you think?"

"Greg's got the means."

"Here's what makes more sense to me," Katie said. "The overseas companies he's got his fingers in fell into some trouble. He brings in my firm to fix them, realizes that it's me they're sending, and then maybe decides to fly out a little early just in case."

"And was he right to fly out? *Just in case?*"

Here's where I wasn't sure how to answer. The honest answer was no, so I tried that.

"Good answer. There's something…off about that couple. Ever since he showed up in Hong Kong…" She shook her head. "Everything's different. I don't see the man I saw in him before."

I thought about Chloe and her persistence. "I know what you mean."

Katie took a deep breath. I knew that look; she was about to say something I wasn't going to be happy with. "So here's the thing. I can finish poking around at a few things from here, but to confirm my suspicions, I need to go back to Hong Kong."

I didn't love the idea of losing her again, but I felt like this was the home stretch. "Right. Of course."

Katie bit her lip. "The timing'll mean I'll miss the soft opening of the new bar." She blew out a sigh. "And maybe the grand opening, too."

Katie had been with me through the opening of all of my other bars. She was my constant. This one was named after her, for God sakes. And now she wasn't going to make the opening?

Reading my expression, she reached across the table and touched my hand. "I'll try to make it home, honey. But I have to do this. It's now or I may miss this opportunity."

I turned my hand over and squeezed hers back. "I understand, Kates. Do what you need to do."

Katie was home for just over a week before we were driving her back to the airport. We made love every night, but things felt strained. The rational part of my brain told me that there was no reason to be worried. That Chloe was full of it and that everything Katie had told me was true. There was no reason for her to lie.

But details nagged. When Katie shared photos she'd taken from her room, I thought about how Chloe knew about that view, too. Had Greg been up there? I thought about Katie's exchange with Nadia and how pleasantly they seemed to get along, despite their past "rivalry."

I should have asked about these things. That's what Katie would have done. But I had the opening of The Katherine on my mind, filling my days and nights, and I had to remember to be a father and husband in that time, too.

Just a little longer, I kept reassuring myself. Pushing it off. Delaying the inevitable. When we dropped Katie off at the airport, the soft opening was Thursday. Grand opening was Friday. Less than a week, and everything could go back to normal.

"This'll be quick. A couple nights, tops," Katie said. We kissed. "Max, trust me. Okay?"

"I trust you. Good luck, honey."

Just one more week and all would be well. So why did I keep thinking that everything was about to go terribly wrong?

****

Soft opening a restaurant was mostly about training the staff, making sure everything goes smoothly before the grand opening to the public (and to the critics). Soft opening a bar was more about buzz. The invitees comprised bloggers, journalists, local celebrities, and moneyed clientele—influencers in the community who'd start a buzz once the bar opened to everyone.

It was also my least favorite part of opening a bar. I hated schmoozing—not because of the socializing. You couldn't be a successful bartender, let alone bar owner, and not be comfortable with socializing. But I hated mixing with people just to get something from them. It was why I hired a firm to handle my PR.

Tomorrow night's opening, the one to the public and my real customers, was much more satisfying. I could blend in there. Listen to what they said. What they liked. And get a much more genuine critique.

After dropping Mya off at my parents, I stopped by The Katherine to do one final inspection. A few people were already here, preparing for the opening. They looked up at me and nodded. I nodded back. We all had a job to do and we were all focused on doing the best we could.

It was a narrow space with a long bar down the left side and private booths along the right. I'd used The James as inspiration, although this place was far more polished than her grittier bar.

The chairs were all up on the tables, the stools resting on the top of the lacquered bar (save for one spot where the bartender was practicing making cocktails). A few people were going through the place, putting the finishing decorations up.

I took a deep breath. Smelled like paint and lumber. Smelled like hard work.

My phone rang. Chloe. A chill ran up my spine.

"Hello, Chloe."

"Hello yourself, stranger. You give Katie a good homecoming?"

I wondered if she knew that my wife was onto her husband. Judging from that tone, I doubted it. "We had a good time."

"And now she's back in Hong Kong. With Greg. Just like that. I knew she'd accept his invitation."

"What?"

"Didn't she tell you why she was headed out there?" Chloe asked.

Now there was an awkward question to answer. *To bust your husband's criminal ways?* Luckily, it was also a rhetorical one.

"He wanted someone to be his date for this celebratory reception at one of his latest acquisitions. Hold on, let me text you a photo of them just before it started."

A moment later, my phone buzzed and in came a pic of my wife and Greg. He wore a tuxedo. She wore a long evening gown that I'd never seen. Everything about her screamed elegance, from her make-up to the way her hair was styled to the chandelier earrings. I would have killed to have her on my arm looking like that tonight, and she was thousands of miles away on someone else's.

"I need have too much shit on my plate to deal with right now, Chloe. I need to go."

I pressed *end*, cutting her laugh off sharply.

"Hey, Max," said the bartender. "Can you taste this? I'm still getting the hang of using egg whites in drinks. I can't tell if it's off, or just in my head."

"Sure," I said, happy to do something other than worry about what the hell Katie was doing. "What is it?"

"It's the Pisco Sour," he said, holding the drink up. The milky yellow concoction had a frothy white head on it.

"Looks authentic." Taking it from him, I tipped the drink back and drank it down like lemonade on a hot day. "Tastes about right. Nice job."

Behind him, the door to the back swung open and the three-piece jazz-band struggled in. "Want us to set up back here?" a beefy guy holding a cello case asked.

Business called. Thank God for that.

"Hold on, I'll show you where to put that down." To the bartender, I said, "Make me another. Let's make sure we get it right."

Why wouldn't she have told me about the reception? Where did she get that dress? That jewelry? How could she look so fucking happy standing next to a guy she said creeped her out?

But how could I be mad? I mean really, how? I was no innocent bystander in this game. It had been my obsession that had kicked it off. I never even considered that Katie would take it where she did, but I was ultimately the master of my own demise.

Nadia found me more than a little tipsy by mid-afternoon. Sampling cocktails—even when after limiting myself to a couple sips—had my head spinning. I needed it, though. It was that or go crazy with jealousy and anger.

"You need to go home and crash, Max. And sober up. You need

to be your sharpest when I throw you to the wolves."

"Don't worry about me. I'll be fine," I said. At least I wasn't slurring.

"You'll be fine after a nap. Now go. I'll take care of the rest here."

"You've always been good to me. Why didn't I notice that?"

Nadia snorted a laugh. "You were too busy looking at my ass. Now go!"

****

Nadia was right. Two hours of rest really did do wonders. It also required me to run around like crazy preparing for tonight. I had just enough time to shower, shave, and dress. No time to think. No time to worry. All that was behind me. Or ahead. Right now, I needed to be *on*.

I was at the door when they opened for the first time to customers—not the public, not quite yet, but in many ways, tonight's test was harder than tomorrow's. I opted not to go with a gangster outfit. That felt too much like a costume to me, and while many of the guys in attendance favored the black suit, tie, and fedora look, I wasn't here to perform but to reinforce a mood.

"Make note of this, Nadia, but this is the first time I've ever felt under dressed in a tuxedo."

Nadia pretended to scribble something down on her clipboard. "Noted."

Nadia was draped in a short, silver and black dress with silver heels that wrapped around her ankles and lower calves. With her hair tight and back and fixed in place with a simple headband, the exotic—and obviously foreign—beauty pulled off the modern flapper better than most here.

"Careful where your eyes wander, boss," Nadia said. The dress hung low enough to make her plump cleavage too tempting to resist looking. "That's for paying customers, only."

I laughed. "Get back to work."

"Yes, sir."

I greeted. I schmoozed. I smiled at all the right people, wandering from group to group so that no one felt excluded. Yet I couldn't kick the feeling of being alone.

"Where's your wife this evening, dear?" The wife of one of the city's leading philanthropists asked the question but she hadn't been the first. We'd met a number of times, and the older woman was always kind to me, but I could never remember her name.

"She's in China, actually, on business. She sends her regrets."

"That's too bad. She's always such a bright spot at these dreadful events." Then, remembering who I was, waved the insult away like it was nothing. "Not your new bar. It's delightful. Just...these people."

We shared a laugh. "Oh, I know just what you mean. I'll tell Katie you said hi."

"Do."

And it was on to the next cluster of people, although the old woman's words lingered. *Always such a bright spot...* Katie wasn't just that, but she gave all of this meaning. Talking to these people that I didn't care about? It felt pointless if I couldn't share a laugh with her later on about it, and even more pointless when I considered the possibility that I'd *never* share the stories with her again.

Life without Katie was meaningless. I decided then and there that no matter what, I had to get her back.

"Alone at last," came a familiar voice. I picked up her vanilla perfume a moment before I felt her hands on my shoulders. "You're a busy man."

"Chloe!"

"Thanks for the invite. Greg sends his regrets. He's too busy with his cock in your wife's beautiful little cunt." She circled me, staying close.

Chloe did the Prohibition Era thing with sass. She was more reminiscent of classic Hollywood than a flapper. Her blonde hair was crimped, she wore fat pearls around her slender neck, and her dress was short, sequined, and sexy.

"Welcome to The Katherine."

"Cute name. I wonder what the real Katherine's doing right now..." Chloe smiled over the lip of her martini.

"I'm sure she's doing well."

"I think we both know how well she's doing. We've both seen it before, haven't we?"

No amount of alcohol could make my head buzz like Chloe's words were now. "Chloe…"

"There are a lot of things she's never told you, Max." Her hand ran across the front of my pants. "Your wife is a slut."

The word snapped me out of my spell. I stepped back. "Don't call her that."

Chloe's eyebrows went up. "No? But she is, Max. Last time I checked, only sluts sleep around behind their husbands' backs."

"That puts you in that category," I said. The hackles on the back of my neck were up.

"I never claimed I wasn't. All I'm suggesting is that why hold back anymore, Max? Katie's so willing to try a little strange when you're not looking. Why not join her?"

"How do I know you're not just making it all up?"

Chloe ignored the question, asking one of her own. "Did you know that Hong Kong wasn't the first time they got together behind your back? They've been meeting ever since the art opening. Didn't you suspect?"

"No—"

"Oh yes. All those lunches you thought she was having with me? Most of the time, they were actually getting together and fooling around. We did have lunch a couple times, though, and she told me she couldn't get enough of Greg's cock."

"Why are you telling me this now? Why didn't you tell me before?" And why didn't Katie tell me? Despite myself, my cock was alive, but this time, that sense of betrayal was stronger. If she'd just been truthful with me, this situation could have been so fucking hot. All of it. If Katie had just let me in, then it would have been perfect. Why wouldn't she?

"Because you need to hear the truth. Because I'm getting tired of waiting for you to see it yourself. You've blinded yourself for too long, Max. You know that guy John? Her coworker? She's been sleeping with him, too. She told me that they've been lovers since last year. You never suspected?"

My voice steadied. "No."

"I'm sorry to be the one to tell you, but—"

"No, Chloe. It's over. Please, just stop."

Misinterpreting what I was saying, she stepped close, shifting from dealing pain to doling out sympathy in frightening succession. "I'm sorry, Max, but it'll be okay. Let me take care of you."

I pushed her back. "I said no, Chloe. Just stop, before I make a scene."

The blonde blinked. "Excuse me?"

"Let me rephrase." My breath trembled with anger. "I want you to turn around, walk out that door, and never come back into my life. Again."

"I know you're upset at Katie, but don't take it out on me—"

"Chloe, I'll ask you one more time. If you don't leave now, I'm going to have security escort you out."

A few people had stopped, taking notice of us. The scene had started, and as bad as this would be for PR, I wasn't going to stop it if that's what it required. Chloe saw the eyes on her, too, then saw the tenacity in my own.

"Fine, but this conversation isn't over." She tucked her clutch purse under her arm and sauntered out, the crowd parting around her like she was radioactive.

Oh, but it is, I said to myself.

"You okay, Max?" Nadia was there at my side, a hand on my shoulder to calm me.

"Yeah." But I wasn't. I felt light-headed, like I was about to faint.

"Sit down. Here, on the stool. Right here. And breathe."

The world closed up around me, a tiny pinprick of light. I felt padding beneath me. A stool. And water against my lips.

"Drink. Drink. And breathe."

When I opened my eyes (when had I even shut them?), a crowd had gathered, faces filled with curiosity and concern.

"He's fine. Just had a little too much to drink," Nadia said to the crowd. "See, even the owner isn't immune to the effects of absinthe. Drink responsibly, all."

I hadn't been drinking absinthe, but as Nadia's words worked their way through the crowd and the story traveled, I hoped that the bartenders had boned up on their absinthe drinks. She'd probably just sold out half our supply right there.

"That fucking bitch," was the first words I spoke when the crowd had dispersed and I was alone with Nadia.

"Yeah," she agreed. "I caught the last things she said. None of it's true, you know. The stuff with John and Katie? Couldn't have happened. He would have told me."

"Can you trust him?"

Nadia shot me a sardonic smile, as if to say, *Are you fucking kidding me?* "Yeah, I can trust him. That's our understanding. That's the only way it works with us. If we can't trust each other, how the hell can we love each other?"

I thought about Greg's opinion on this. How he got off on not knowing what his wife was up to. How that had slowly become the norm in my head. I started to realize how tightly wrapped in Chloe's web I was. Something about that made me laugh.

"What?" Nadia asked, more nervous at my mirth than anything else.

"She warned me. Chloe, I mean. One of the first things she ever said to me was *you can't trust me.* She also said something to the effect of, *I always get what I want.*"

"She wanted you." Nadia shared my laughter. "Like you needed anything else to go to your head."

"Hey, now. I'm not that bad."

Nadia's laughter petered out, but she continued to smile. "No, you're not. Unfortunately for me and Chloe."

"Now who's filling up my head?"

"I'm sorry. Force of habit." We looked out over the bar. The crowd had thinned, but the vibe was good. This place was going to make it. The Katherine was going to make it. Now, I just hoped Katie and I would, too.

"Hey, Max, there's one other thing. I wasn't going to mention it tonight, but in light of what just happened..."

I didn't think I could take any more revelations, but with a line like that, I couldn't let it go. "Go on."

"It's not bad, actually. Well, not in the end. I did some looking into it—actually, I mentioned all this to John, and he did some digging—"

"You told John about Katie and I?"

Nadia looked chagrined for possibly the first time since I'd known her. "Sorry? But this story has a good ending?"

"Every other woman I've come into contact with lately has betrayed me. I guess it's your turn."

Nadia rolled her eyes. "How dramatic, Max. And Katie hasn't betrayed you. Just shut up and listen and we'll get to that. So John did some digging and found out that a Mr. Gregory Reynolds invested a lot of money into their accounting firm right after the federal audit. He may have single-handedly been part of what helped it succeed, when everyone thought it was done."

My mind jumped ahead, quickly connected the dots. "The Hong Kong trip—"

"Wasn't a coincidence that it came right after your night out with them."

"Son of a bitch." Katie was vulnerable. We hadn't talked about what had happened. She was ripe for the seduction. "I'm going to kill him."

"I think that after Katie's done with him, you won't have to. John passed that on as soon as he found out—sometime last week?"

"Why didn't she tell me?"

"Probably because she didn't want you trying to go out and kill him." Nadia patted my knee. "Anyway, that was like the last piece of the puzzle she needed. Did she tell you about the money laundering?"

"Yeah."

"She has most of the evidence she needs to damn him, but she's going for the smoking gun."

"A confession," I said. Suddenly, I thought of her dress and the way Greg had his arm around her. How far would she go to get that confession? "This fucking sucks, you know?"

"What does?" Nadia asked.

"Being stuck here. I feel powerless."

"Trust her, Max. She's got your interests at heart." Nadia rose. "Oh, and I wouldn't trust a single thing that blonde slut says."

"She said they've been fucking for months. At the very least, he's been at her side for weeks."

"Doesn't mean anything," Nadia insisted.

"She had a picture," I said.

"Did it show sex? Did it show anything actually bad?"

"His arm was around her?" Nadia stared at me flatly and I conceded. "You're right, we were set up."

"But your wife was too clever for them, it seems," Nadia said. It was weird hearing her speak about Katie with admiration. "For a guy as business savvy as Greg, he misplayed this one completely."

"Yeah." I stood, and it felt like a rebirth. Everywhere around me, people were having a good time. They were pouring over the complex drink menus. They were tucked in private alcoves feeling a touch clandestine. They were experiencing something forbidden, while playing within the rules.

"Thank you, Nadia." I caught her off-guard with my bear hug. Despite our ongoing flirtation, we didn't physically touch very much. "Thank you for everything."

"I'm just the messenger." She laughed. "But I'm happy to take all the credit."

CHAPTER 12

In the early hours of Saturday morning, when everyone had cleaned up and closed down the bar and I was alone, just me and The Katherine, I got the most unexpected of calls. I almost didn't answer, I was so stunned. But then, how could I not?

"Hello, Greg."

"It's over."

"What's over?" My chest tightened before I could process his words. I skipped understanding, jumping right to that bestial thing that strained to get free. "Stay away from my wife."

"I will, Max. I promise. I'm calling to tell you that I'm sorry. For everything. Not that it matters anymore, but it was never my plan. To seduce you and Katie. That was Chloe the whole time."

"You're right, it doesn't matter." If he'd been standing in front of me, he'd have a broken jaw right now. I could practically feel my knuckles crunching against that All-American face.

"We never slept together out here. She wanted me to tell you that."

"I know." And then I realized that I'd known all along.

"I'm sorry, Max. I really am. I never meant for it to come to this."

"You never wanted to get caught, you mean," I corrected.

Silence hung on the other end of the line.

"It's late here, and I've got a big day tomorrow," I said at last.

"I understand. But I had to call."

"You did." My confidence greeted me like a long lost friend. *Hey, man.* "But don't ever call again. Not me, and not my wife. Understand?"

"I understand. Like I said, it's over. And truly, Max, I'm sorry."

"Goodbye."

Pressing *end* on that call was more than symbolic, but when my phone went black, I knew there was another I needed to call.

Katie's phone went right to voicemail. I started to hang up, but as I listened to Katie's recorded voice apologizing for missing me, then the beep at the end, I started talking anyway.

"Kates, I love you. And I'm so sorry about...so many things. I'm sorry I brought Chloe and Greg into our lives. I'm sorry I didn't trust you more. I'm sorry that we let it get to this point, where I have to leave a message on your phone rather than look you in the eyes and tell you in person."

I took a deep, wavering breath. Tears gathered in my eyes before I brushed them away.

"But I'm not sorry that I got to discover this new side of you— of us. I don't regret sharing my fantasy with you, and watch you live it out. That was awesome. We just picked our partners poorly.

"I'm sorry that you're going to miss the opening It'll be weird without you here for that, but you know what? It'll be here the next day, and the day after that, and the day after that. I love you, Katie. See you when I see you."

I hung up as a tear carved a trail down my cheek. Blinking, I was in The Katherine once again, alone and lost in the dark. It would be here for her. And so would I.

****

The next day—the day of the grand opening—I actually slept in. Maybe it was the fact that I'd gotten such shitty sleep leading up to that night. Maybe it was the emotional exhaustion of the soft opening and all the Chloe and Greg revelations. Maybe I was finally at peace. The rest was out of my hands.

Whatever the reason, I didn't even open my eyes until almost noon. And when I woke up, I felt rested for the first time in ages.

My phone didn't have any messages. No missed calls. It wasn't a great feeling, but I tried not to linger on it.

I stopped by my parents' house to spend some time with Mya. We went to the neighborhood park where I pushed her on the swing.

"Where's mommy, daddy?"

"She's away," I said.

"She's on a trip. She'll be back soon." I clung to the certainty in Mya's statement.

"She will. She will."

The rest of the day passed in a blink. I brushed up on a few of the more popular cocktails from last night, although this time I didn't taste-test them beyond a sip.

Unlike the pre-launch party, I spent my opening nights incognito. I left the ribbon-cutting and first toasts to the manager—Nadia for the second time—while I prowled the crowds. It was much easier to find out what people really thought about your bar when they didn't know it was your bar.

I didn't deliberately disguise myself. People who knew me knew not to make a big deal out of who I was. To everyone else, I was just another bartender, or patron enjoying a successful opening night.

We opened at 9. By 9:30, we had a line.

"It's good," Nadia said. I'd stepped out from behind the bar and eased myself onto a stool that gave me a view of the narrow space. "So far, it's really good."

The buzz was positive. People liked being part of something that felt illicit. Prohibition may have been dead, but The Katherine made you think otherwise. At least for a moment. "Are we turning many away?"

"Not many. A few came by in tennis shoes and t-shirts, but most of the crowd knows the score. Word spread about the dress code."

Word-of-mouth was like electricity: transferring from person to person seamlessly. They brought that excitement in here, charging the air with a level of energy I couldn't have paid for. I felt it, too: a underlying hum that put me on edge, ready for anything.

I closed my eyes. The hum of conversation pounded relentlessly. "I thought absinthe was illegal," I heard the pretty blonde seated behind me say to her equally attractive Asian friend. They were drinking a champagne and absinthe cocktail ominously called a "Death in the Afternoon."

"Me too," the Asian woman whispered. "Let's order another before this place gets shut down."

Absinthe had been legal in the U.S. since 2007, but I liked that they thought they were getting away with something. They'd share that excitement with their friends, who'd come seeking more of the same. That was what this place was all about.

I pushed off my stool and floated through the crowd, capturing snippets of conversation like an impatient man turning the dial on a radio.

"Wow, that's really good."

"Smell the bouquet on this punch."

"I feel like Gatsby."

Nadia was right. So far, it was good. Really good. And that wasn't even counting all the rave reviews I'd previewed in the blogosphere from last night. The Katherine was going to be my most successful bar yet. But something was missing: its namesake.

"Call her?" Nadia was there once again, materialized like a sexy version of my subconscious when I needed her most.

"What?" I asked dumbly.

"Call her," Nadia repeated. "Couldn't hurt, right?"

"She's not going to answer."

"So then she doesn't answer." Nadia leaned closer. "*Call her.*"

I rolled my eyes, but pulled out my phone and called Katie. My wife answered on the second ring.

"Hi." Her achingly familiar voice cut through the noise. Wherever she was, it was as loud as my own surroundings.

"Katie!?"

"Did you mean to call someone else?" I savored the sound of her laugh, wishing I could record it and play it back again and again.

"Where are you?" I asked, plugging the ear not pressed against the phone. "Sounds loud."

"I'm in a bar."

I imagined glitzy Hong Kong around her, an exotic redhead in a sea of dark hair. "I miss you. I wish you were here."

"Oh, Max… So did Greg call you?"

"Yeah."

"They won't be bothering us any more. Not if they want to stay out of jail."

"You didn't have to do that alone, you know, Katie. I could have helped…" I'm not sure how, but I just knew I could have.

"Of course you could have," she humored me, "but it was so much easier this way. And besides, I had help. John was instrumental. What's most important is that they're history."

"And you and I?"

"Still have a lot of history to write, I hope," she said.

"We do." I wished I could hold her in my arms and nuzzle my cheek along hers.

"I got your message. So you like my naughty side?" she asked.

My body grew hot. My cock reacted. "I do."

"Good, because I don't think it'd be easy to just ignore." Her voice sounded so close. I jammed the phone harder against my skull. "And I don't think you want me to ignore it, either."

I gulped, but didn't say anything.

"I'm looking at a pretty hot guy here right now. I think he may be game for a little fun."

Jealousy twisted knots in my gut, but my erection raged. The drug was back. The draw of the forbidden that would never be fully satisfied.

"Just a little fun?" I said, my voice steady despite the way I felt. "Wrong guy then."

Her response didn't come through the phone line. I heard it right against my ear, feeling hot breath and a woman's touch encircle me from behind. "Maybe I can convince him to be more than a little naughty."

I almost dropped my phone. I turned, finding Katie standing before me, her wide smile a mirror of my own. "You're here."

"*Finally*," she agreed. "I've been flying for the past 36 hours. I'm so tired of foreign airports and shitty food."

"Flying?" I did the math. So that's why she'd been off her phone. Not because she was with someone else, or that she was mad, but that—

"Are you going to keep standing there and over-thinking the situation, or are you going to kiss your wife hello?"

I did just that, pulling her close and sliding my lips into place against hers. The kiss was one I'd been dreaming of for days now—a kiss that I was worried I'd never share again. It came from somewhere deep inside of us, born from years of love and familiarity, yet delivered with the same freshness as our first. They say absence makes the heart grow fonder, but they didn't say anything about the kisses being so fucking good.

"Get a room, you two."

Nadia crossed her arms as she leaned onto the bar.

"You knew she was here," I said to her.

Nadia smirked. "I also knew that she'd been trying to get home for the past two days, but this makes it worth it."

"Thanks for looking out for him, Nadia," Katie said. She still hadn't stepped out of my embrace, and I wasn't about to let her go quite so easily.

"Hey, watching Max is one of my favorite pastimes," Nadia said before she could help it. "I mean, not that anything would ever happen...um..."

Katie just laughed. "That's too bad. I was trying to think of creative ways to thank you and John, and you just eliminated the top contender."

Nadia and I were both stunned. I stared at Katie, the woman whose jealousy could be so intense that I'd gotten into the habit of not mentioning Nadia's name even in a business context.

"What?" Katie giggled. "Don't tell me that you two haven't wanted to jump each other for years."

"I think she's fucking with us," I said to Nadia, but couldn't be sure.

"I'll show you some fucking," Katie said. She pulled me toward the back, asking Nadia over her shoulder, "This way to the office?"

Nadia grinned and nodded her head. Her dark eyes followed us until the crowd swallowed us up.

****

"I missed you so much." Katie sighed as we melted into one another's arms. "I love you, Maxwell Callahan, and for a second, I thought I'd lost you."

"I'm right here."

I pulled back, studying her for the first time that night. She wore a red, single-shouldered dress that was so seamless it looked poured on. The brocaded detailing around her shoulders gave it a hint of the Roaring 20s and her make-up was glamorous to match, but nothing about her look suggested someone trying too hard.

I brushed a strand of red hair from her freckled cheeks. She'd worn in down in long, coppery waves that cascaded around her shoulders as she leaned back onto the desk.

"I'm sorry again about Chloe and Greg," I said. "I never should have given you her card."

"But you did because you wanted to open up our relationship."

"No," was my first instinct. That sounded awful, but in a way, it was true, too. "Okay, yes. And that's why I really feel terrible."

Katie mirrored my touch, reaching out to run her hand along my cheek. "Don't. They were a dangerous couple to be our first, but we survived."

"Our first?" My cock was at full attention.

"Less talk. More getting reacquainted," she said. Her kiss followed, her soft touch on my cheek growing firm.

My hands strayed down her dress, silky smooth under my palms. I felt the back strap of her bra and the faintest hint of her tiny panties, and something else.

Hoisting her up onto the edge of the desk, I pushed the hem of her dress up her leg, discovering the lacy fringe of her nude stockings, then the strap of her garter belt.

"You like it?" she asked. "I felt they were Era appropriate."

I glanced at the lingerie. It was blood red as her dress. "Good thing. Wouldn't want to have to throw you out."

"Well, I'm no historian, but I don't think many women wore g-strings in the 1920s, so you may need to throw me out anyway."

"Good thing my stance on bribes is Era appropriate, too," I said.

"Are you suggesting that I can stay if I suck your cock?"

The question emerging from the old Katie was unthinkable. Or maybe it had been there all along, ready to emerge. Either way, she was here to stay.

"I'm afraid this offense is far more serious." I loosened my belt and lifted her legs up onto the desk. With my cock in one hand, I stepped close, pushing the gusset of her g-string to the side. "We at The Katherine take historical anachronisms very seriously."

"About that name—UH!"

Her pussy accepted my thrust without resistance. She wrapped her legs around me and leaned back on her desk. "How does it make you feel, being part of something so illicit?"

A sweep of auburn hair fell across her eyes, making her look even more the part of the temptress. "I love it."

I pulled down the side of her dress not supported with the single strap, revealing a lacy red bra that just barely covered her nipple. I freed that a moment later, tweaking it with my thumb.

"Of course you do, you little slut."

The term felt like a blow from me to her. I cringed even as it left my mouth, only to feel her pussy ripple around me.

"I'm *your* little slut, though. No one else's. Remember that." She tossed her head, dislodging the hair from her face momentarily. "God, it's been too long. You feel so big."

"I saw the photo of you and Greg before that reception. You were hot." I let her think about that. "So you didn't seduce him into a confession?"

"Oh, I seduced him into a confession. But he got nothing out of it."

"Nothing?"

"Well, maybe a kiss." She giggled as she felt me surge inside her. "Really? Even with all we've been through?"

"I can't help what makes me hot." I pumped her a few times. "And you can't, either. You weren't at all tempted to try his big dick one more time?"

"I wasn't. Seriously." She let her breath catch up to her, then gave up trying when she couldn't. "Even if I could overlook the sleaze-factor, he was actually just too big to be really good."

"So you're saying this is all you need?" My sarcasm was mild. I knew she wasn't just telling me that to make me feel better about my above-average cock.

"That and the man attached to it." She drew me in for a long, sweet kiss. "But I'm not saying that I don't *want* to try more."

I sped up my pumping hips, driving down as Katie began to bounce hers up. "Have anyone in mind?"

"Well, now that you mention it, I hear Nadia and John are pretty open-minded," she said.

My balls seized as a new fantasy formed out of an old one. "You'd like that, wouldn't you? You'd finally be able to finish seducing that quiet young man, and one-up Nadia at the same time."

"Stop living in the past, Max." Katie's nails dug into the back of my neck as her orgasm eclipsed her. With the last bits of breath she had, she said, "I want to fuck her, too."

I saw the future in our mutual orgasm. It was a bright one, filled with new adventures and lightning-hot experiences. It wouldn't be without challenges. We'd probably have a few more Greg and Chloes. But we'd have them together, and each time, we'd grow from them.

But right now, tonight, the grand opening of The Katherine, we were all about celebration. And as I buried myself in Katie's tight embrace and we came down from our lust-fueled high, I realized that the celebration had only just begun.

****

I emerged from the back alone, half-expecting the entire bar to be staring at me in judgment. No one gave me a second glance.

I spotted John seated at the bar, checking his phone. A wide-mouthed glass blooming with fruit sat in front of him. Nadia was up at the front, talking with the host staff, so I slid in behind the bar and approached her husband.

"Hey, John. Glad you could make it."

He looked up at me, his smile boyish and shy as always. "Hey, Max. I'm glad I could, too."

"Hey, thanks for helping us," I said. "With the whole mess, I mean. Never thought we'd get mixed up with a pair of psycho swingers."

John waved the gratitude away like it was nothing. "All I did was relay some information."

"It was some pretty critical information, though." We shared a laugh and that was that: I said my piece, he said his, and we moved on. I pointed at his drink. "You don't like it?"

"It's certainly very...fruity. I didn't realize that when I ordered a punch."

"It's there for the smell, not so much to be eaten," I explained. I spotted Katie out of the corner of my eye. She squeezed in at the end of the bar and glanced over the drink menu.

"Check out the chick in red," I said. "She's had her eye on you all night."

At first, John was confused. Following my eyes, he got the game I was playing. "You sure?"

"Actually, you're right. She's had her eye on you long before tonight." I nodded, pulling out a couple saucer-style champagne glasses and a shaker. "And from what your wife has told me, the attraction's mutual."

"So that's what that text was about," he said to himself. "We've never done anything."

"Good." I shook up a drink, poured it into the two glasses, and pushed them before him. "Let's fix that tonight. Give her one of these. Tell her the bartender recommended it."

For a guy who was no stranger to stranger-sex, John looked like I'd announced that I was Santa Claus and that Christmas was starting *right now*. For a long moment, I didn't think he was going to take it. He looked at the drinks, pale yellow and brimming with promise, then back up at me. At last, he scooped them up and turned to go with a nod.

"What are they called, in case she asks?" he said over his shoulder.

"The Last Word."

Watching John thread his way through the thick crowd at the bar gave me the now-familiar jitters. We were headed into new territory once again. Dangerous territory, yet safely so.

Nadia took John's place on the opposite side of the bar. She plucked a piece of pineapple out of his abandoned punch and bit into it before looking up at me. "What are you up to?"

I watched as John stepped up behind Katie, tapped her on the shoulder, and offered her the drink. She smiled, looked surprised, then glanced in our direction. Our eyes met, her connection as clear to me as if she'd whispered it right against my ear: *You sure?*

I nodded, then looked back at Nadia. "So I have this fantasy that involves my wife and other men..."

EPILOGUE

"Oh, yes. Right...there!" We could hear Katie's voice pour from the bedroom all the way at the base of the stairs. The stairs of our home. Even in the dark, I could see the family photos walk up the shadow-splashed walls. Not that I was actually seeing any of them. All my focus was on upstairs. On Katie's moans.

For the owner and the manager to leave the opening night of a new bar an hour early would have been unthinkable. Missing what was happening in that bedroom would have been impossible.

It was 1:30. Katie and John had left a half hour ago. I was proud of myself that I'd held out as long as I had. It was one of the longest half-hours of my life.

"Uh, yeah. Fuck...me. Fuckme!" Katie's cries burned in my ears. I glanced back at Nadia, trailing me on the stairs. Her eyelids flashed open. She nodded.

They were in the master bedroom, the door left wide. I froze just inside the doorframe as the debauchery of the scene crashed home.

Katie rode John reverse cowgirl, her heaving nudity in my direct line of sight. She'd left the red garter belt and nude stockings on, framing the lewd scene before me. Otherwise, nothing was hidden. Not the way her tits spilled over the lacy top of her crimson bra, hard nipples screaming. Not the way John clutched her hips as he fucked her from beneath, or the pale pink latex of his condom. I could even see the outline of his cock head stretch Katie's smooth waxed pussy lips as he withdrew, the ridge dragging along her g-spot.

"Oh my God, that feels good." Katie planted her arms straight back and arched her chest to the ceiling. The cups of her bra slipped lower down her torso, releasing her full breasts.

John moved his right hand off Katie's hip, sliding it down between her legs. Following the dart of auburn curls, he fingered Katie's clit in time with his thrusting cock.

"That's so fucking hot," Nadia whispered against my ear. I was suddenly aware of the other woman, pressed close behind me, watching over my shoulder. "Natural redhead, too. I always wondered."

I didn't say a word. Couldn't. Not with the sight before me. This may be something Nadia and John were used to, but it was only the second time for me.

"Are you okay?" Nadia asked.

Heat bloomed across my face, shame and excitement fueling that fire. "Yeah."

"Just yeah? Or *fuck yeah*?" Her hand caressed my hard on before I could answer. "Fuck yeah it is."

It felt like déjà vu, being led into a room like that. One day,

I needed to see the initial stages of seduction—now that I knew there'd be a one-day. To watch Katie strip a man, and be stripped, would be something to savor.

"Oh, fuck, I'm come—ming!" Katie cried.

Not that I was complaining about the current setup.

Nadia's whisper reminded me that I was not alone. "Mind if I join them?"

I shook my head, not trusting my voice. The brunette detached herself from me and sauntered into the room. I leaned against the doorframe, working up the courage to follow.

"It's about time you two got it on," Nadia said, announcing herself to the fucking couple. Katie was still in the grips of her orgasm to care. John just looked around Katie and smiled at his wife.

Nadia pulled her black blouse over her head, revealing a matching black bra. Her skirt went next, revealing a pair of thigh-highs and a black thong.

John rolled Katie to the side as she came down from her panting high. She curled up onto her side, her closed eyes and wide smile pure bliss. Nadia crawled onto the bed opposite her, her mouth seeking out John's.

I thought back to Chloe and Greg and our wild hotel foursome, and try as I might, I couldn't remember the two of them ever sharing a kiss—and certainly not like the one Nadia and John shared. Nadia pulled away at one point, her whisper just loud enough to reach my ears.

"I love you so much, baby. And I've missed you..."

John looked pained. "I'm trying to get back, honey. I think I've got a lead."

Nadia rolled her panties down and climbed into his lap. "Well, you're here now. Let's make the most of it."

Her bra came off as she settled onto John's cock. I watched the muscles in her back tighten and flex as she arched over him, the long sweep of tawny skin a work of art.

Beside them, Katie shifted, coming back to herself. She found me standing in the door. Nothing else mattered but that smile. She reached out for me and I went to her and sat on the edge of the bed.

Her voice was hoarse. "You saw me?"

"I watched, yeah. You were sexy."

"And you're not mad?"

"Never. I'm glad you two got to finally cross that line."

Katie laughed. "You know, not all lines are meant to be crossed, Max."

I loosened my tie, pulling it over my head without fully unfastening it. I started working on the buttons of my shirt as Katie fumbled with my belt. "I know, but some are inevitable."

My shirt came off at the same time that Katie freed my cock. I rolled her onto her back and crawled over her as she pushed my trousers down with her toes. They snagged on my ankles, but I was too impatient to care.

Her pussy welcomed me home, warm and ready to receive. Our bodies were as one, eyes locked, skin on skin. "That feels good, Max. Just right."

She'd now been with two other men since our adventure had begun—and I was pretty sure that the future would hold more—but nothing would compare to this connection. I knew it as surely as I knew Katie loved me. It helped with the jealousy and insecurity. It helped still that restless turmoil in my gut—*still* but not *eliminate*. I knew now that those emotions were as much a part of this fantasy as the excitement.

"Look at them, John," Nadia said.

The lens of my consciousness drew back. For a moment, I felt distant from myself, a man on a bed with three others. Katie and I weren't alone. John was there, lying next to her, Nadia hunched over him.

"It's beautiful," John agreed.

"Can we be like that one day?" Nadia asked.

I drifted back to myself, rejoining the scene with a snap.

John reached up and touched his wife's face. "Absolutely."

I looked down at Katie, who smiled at me and shrugged. It was nice to have something that others wanted.

Still to John, Nadia said, "You know what I've always wanted to do?"

John had smile lines around his eyes. I saw the distinguished man he'd be in ten years. Looking at Katie and I, he said, "I see a couple things you've always wanted to do."

Nadia laughed. "Well, one of those is off-limits. The other, I'm still not sure."

With her eyes locked on Katie, Nadia leaned over and kissed my wife.

In the vast catalogue of my fantasies, this one was one of the last I thought I'd ever see. Yet there it was, playing out inches away from me. I was close enough to see their tongues frolic and hear the wet sounds of the kiss.

Nadia brushed her dark hair over her ear, tilting her head—whether to give me a better view or kiss Katie deeper, I couldn't be sure.

John shifted out from under Nadia, freeing the dusky skinned woman to make-out with Katie without the awkward twist of her body. He circled around, re-entering her from behind.

Nadia broke the kiss with a sigh, tossing her head back as she accepting her husband's cock. Katie seized the moment to dribble kisses down the other woman's neck, lingering in the hollow above her clavicle before taking a dark nipple into her mouth.

Nadia's moan rose, then cracked. Her eyes shut, her head back, my body moved on auto-pilot. Still pumping slowly inside my wife, I leaned over and kissed my long-time manager and close friend.

Nadia returned the kiss with hunger. I could feel her shuddering pleasure in the way she kissed. With three of us working her, she didn't last long.

When I pulled away, Katie was there again, kissing the other woman long and deep. "Was it everything you wanted?" Katie demanded. "Do you want to do more than just kiss Max?"

"Uh, yes..." Nadia said.

Katie glanced up at me, her green eyes on fire. "Do you want to fuck him, Nadia? Do you want to feel him pound you?"

I started pumping her harder as she dished her dirty words. Was she teasing Nadia? Was she teasing me...?

"Ngh, yes," Nadia mumbled.

Still looking at me, Katie said, "I want to watch that. I've wanted to see you in action ever since Chloe suggested it. I just didn't want it to be with her."

I nodded, although I still didn't understand. Where was the jealous Katie I'd come to know? Where was the rivalry between her and Nadia that I'd tip-toed around for the last five years?

Katie drew me close, her voice only for me. "I want you to show her how good you are, to show her what will always be mine.

Can you do that for me?"

I understood. I should have understood all along. In so many ways, the impulse was no different than my own. We shared a heated kiss as Nadia climaxed somewhere in the background.

Then, with wordless coordination, John withdrew from Nadia and rolled her on her back. I pulled out, my cock wet and throbbing with anticipation.

The soft yellow light of the bedside lamp caught in the sheen of her sweat, turning Nadia's body into a Bollywood movie star gone bad. Her tits were as perfect as I remembered, full and ripe with youth. Her pussy was the same dusky color as the rest of her, adorned with a manicured brush of dark hair as sexy as her black stay-ups.

I checked on Katie, who just smiled and held up a condom, already unwrapped. She took me into her mouth and gave me a few sucks before rolling on my latex protection.

Katie hugged me from behind as I walked on my knees up to Nadia's supine beauty. My wife reached around, took my cock between her slender fingers, and placed it against Nadia's pussy.

Katie actually moaned as I sank into the other woman, like it was a part of her entering the warm embrace. She let go of my cock once I was in, her fingers dancing across to play with Nadia's clit.

"Does that feel good?" Katie asked. I didn't answer, unsure whether it was for Nadia or I. She thrummed Nadia's clit faster. Her voice came hoarse and strained against my ear. "That's so hot. So hot and so wrong."

I met her in an over the shoulder kiss, although it was nearly impossible to maintain.

"Now I think I understand why you wanted to see me with

another man," she said. "Make her scream. I'll be watching."

She retreated, leaving me to focus on Nadia, the girl of my illicit dreams.

"Hi there," I said, looking down at her. Her dark hair fanned around her in lustrous waves. I folded her knees up against my chest and pumped her deeper.

"Hi, back."

We shared this look, like: *can you fucking believe we're doing this?*

Then I squeezed her calves, folded her in half, and did as my wife ordered. I made her scream.

Nadia careened back into the mattress, head and hair thrashing as we worked out years of sexual build-up. I was right there with her, angling over her, her knees compressed between us.

With my balls clapping against Nadia's ass and her hysterical cries filling my ears, I was so close to coming. I looked over at Katie, who'd arranged herself on John's lap at the head of the bed, his cock once again dancing in and out of her.

She smiled, nodded, and mouthed, *I love you.*

With a hand lazily circling her clit, right above John's buried member, I watched her orgasm consume her. Her breath caught in her throat. Her lips parted. Her eyes closed. Her auburn hair was a mess, darkened with sweat along her brow. One long bang caught in the gloss of her lipstick. The rest hung precariously behind an ear. With one sharp, "Uh!" she crested. It was like watching the sunrise. I was filled with warmth and hope. With love.

I joined her in the moment, burying myself inside Nadia, nuzzling her neck and drinking in her intoxicating aroma. It was the strangest thing, but even though I was with Nadia, I felt like I'd just come with my wife.

****

Katie twirled her fingers through my chest hair as we lay naked in bed. "I think I finally understand how you feel...about me with other men."

Katie and I were alone at last. Morning had come and gone. We'd gotten up and had some cereal, but still had hours before we needed to get Mya, so we'd returned to the bedroom for some one-on-one time.

"You understand? That makes one of us," I said. I still hadn't come to grips with why my wife-sharing fantasy was so strong, but I'd at least come to peace with it.

"When I watched you with Nadia, I felt...well, intensely jealous. The wrongness was so visceral. Like I could practically reach out and touch it. And yet, I can't believe how turned on it made me. It was incredible watching you in action like that. When she screamed, I actually came, too."

"Yeah, watching you with John was like that. It was awesome, and sexy, but I'm not sure I'll ever be able to be completely at ease with it."

"I think that's good," she said, echoing an earlier thought of mine.

"Me, too." I kissed her softly. "But I hope it wasn't the last time."

Katie laughed. "Of course you do." She paused, had the modesty to look a little abashed, and added: "I'm pretty sure it wasn't."

ACKNOWLEDGEMENTS

This book has been a long time coming. I probably had a first draft of this a couple years ago, back when it had a different name and a much different story arc. This was before *Leap* and *Just Watch Me* were even twinkles in my proverbial eye, and those kinds of fantasies (coined "hotwife," although I'm not a fan of the phrase) were in their infancy for me. I wasn't satisfied with the story I'd created in that first draft, so put it on hold and moved on to other ideas. There it waited, ready to be picked up when I'd figured out the story that I wanted to tell. The book you hold in your hands is that story, and I honestly could not do it without the help of a lot of fine friends.

Big thanks to my editor, Lucy V. Morgan, who makes my prose and my plots stronger;

Thanks to Kirsten McCurran, who went above and beyond as a beta reader, and who helped me make this book above and beyond in the process;

Thanks to Max Sebastian, who offered time out of his busy schedule of writing, working, and being a family man to read and comment;

Special thanks to Hal, who read the original story, loved it, and whose words haunted me until I came back to finish it;

And as always a sincere thanks to my wife for her support and all the time that she's allowed me to dedicate in order to write filthy things for all of you.

And of course, thank *you* for reading to the end. I probably wouldn't still be here, plugging away at these books if I didn't have your support. If you *really* want to show your gratitude, drop a review on Amazon, Barnes & Noble, or wherever you purchased this ebook. You have no idea what a good review on those sites does for a guy's ego.

ABOUT THE AUTHOR

I'm just a guy who writes what I like to read: steamy, explicit erotica that's just crazy enough to be true. I write romantic erotica. I write about characters that I like, and endings that feel natural. I write stories where husbands watch their wives get naughty. I write about MILFs and erotic games and loss of innocence. I believe in a world where men read and appreciate erotica, and hope to contribute to it word by word.

Find me online at www.kennywriter.com, or follow me on Twitter at @kennywriter.

ALSO BY KENNY WRIGHT

After School Special (A Short)
All In: Strip Poker Done Right
Eight Hundred Dollar Heels (A Short)
Just Watch Me
Leap
Moving Mrs. Mitchell (A Short)
Naughty But Nice (A Short)
Rediscovering Danielle (A Short)
Something Forbidden
While She Watches
Unconventional (coming soon)

For a full list of titles, along with their covers, synopses, and where to purchase, go to www.kennywriter.com/books.

37541300R00136

Made in the USA
Lexington, KY
06 December 2014